BORN
HUTTERITE

BORN
HUTTERITE

Stories by Samuel Hofer

Canadian Cataloguing in Publication Data
Hofer, Samuel, 1962-
  Born Hutterite
  ISBN 0-9693056-4-8
1. Hutterite Brethren - Fiction. I. Title.
PS8565.0447B6 1991 C813/.54 C91-097082-3
PR9199.3.H644B6 1991

Book design by Samuel Hofer
Cover illustration by Nancy Penner Henn
Edited by Naomi Frankel

Printed and bound by
Houghton Boston, Saskatoon, Canada

Published by:
Hofer Publishers
P.O. Box 9784
Saskatoon, Saskatchewan
S7K 7G5

CONTENTS

INTRODUCTION

When travelling in rural areas of the northern Great Plains, a person may occasionally come upon small distinctive looking clusters of buildings. These buildings, which are usually a short distance from any main highway or road, appear to make up small villages, yet no public roads pass through them. Each of these settlements consists of three to four long, motel-like houses divided into family units, a large kitchen and dining hall building in the centre of the colony, a school, barns, shops and various small sheds. These curious looking communities are home to the Hutterites.

Hutterites are a group of ethnic people who believe that salvation lies in communal living according to Acts 2:44 of the New Testament. The central principle or ethos that keeps their community united is that of owning all things in common in a farming life-style removed from mass society.

With origins stemming from the sixteenth-century Protestant Reformation, Hutterites are one of three surviving Anabaptist groups — the other two are the Mennonites and the Amish — that share a body of common beliefs, including adult or believer's baptism, non-violent resistance or pacifism, and simple living. The Hutterites differ from Amish and Mennonite groups by their practice of communal ownership of property and communal living.

The Hutterite sect was founded in 1528,

when a group of approximately 600 refugees fleeing religious persecution in Nikolsburg, Moravia (today Czechoslovakia) introduced the practice of owning all things in common. Each person heaped his or her private possessions on a cloak that had been spread on the ground; overseers were then selected to manage the goods. The group settled and formed its first *Bruderhof* (place of brethren) at Austerlitz. Since this time, their search for religious freedom has taken Hutterites from Moravia to Slovakia, Hungary, Romania, Russia, the United States and Canada.

The entire group of about 1,265 Hutterites settled in South Dakota, between 1874 and 1879. About half of them chose to settle on homesteading, family-sized farms. These "non-colony" people were called *Prairieleut* (prairie people) by the Hutterites, and they joined with nearby Mennonite groups. Later, in 1918, many of the Hutterites came to Canada when they were harassed by pressure groups upon their refusal to buy war bonds during World War I. Conscientious objectors as they were, some of their men were drafted and sent to army camps, where they were severely starved and beaten. An encounter in which two members died from physical abuses prompted the Hutterites to flee to Canada, and even after legislative changes in the thirties, most remained in Canada.

Hutterites have three distinct subgroups. Each group is like a separate denomination, with its own disciplines, and the groups do not intermarry. The · names of these groups are *Schmiedeleut*, *Dariusleut*, and *Lehreleut*. All originate from the three founding colonies and their leaders in South Dakota. Today the *Shmiedeleut* are exclusively located in Manitoba, North and South Dakota and in Minnesota. The *Dariusleut* and the *Lehreleut* live interspersed in Saskatchewan, Alberta, British Columbia, Montana and Washington. In total, there are approximately 30,000 Hutterites, living in over 300 colonies. Through their distinctive dress — black cloth and suspenders on the men and polka-dot kerchiefs and colourful long skirts for women, they are easily recognized in Great Falls, Winnipeg, Saskatoon, Calgary or Sioux Falls and in many smaller towns in these areas, which they visit frequently.

All Hutterites speak in a Tyrolese German dialect that most nearly resembles that spoken in the province of Carinthia, Austria, that being the area from where the largest number of the original members of the Hutterites were from when they joined the movement in 1762 in Romania. Because this German is an oral, unwritten language, a sprinkling of the present-day vocabulary reflects the Hutterites' stay in Slavic areas, in Transylvania (Romania), in the Ukraine, and in North America. The Tyrolese dialect is primarily used "domestically," in the home. In the church and German school, regular High German is used.

In 1983 I left a Hutterite colony near Moose Jaw, Saskatchewan. My first job away from home was helping build a house on a farm near Regina. After that I was employed on other farms, where I used my farm training and learned willingness to work very hard in order to support myself and attain the goals which had suddenly become possible through my separation from the sheltered life-style of the Hutterite community.

There has always been an inner urge and a need to express myself in some artistic way. Music, art and writing are not encouraged much, are even forbidden, within the Hutterite community. It is believed that such practices are the ways of the world.

In 1989 a non-Hutterite friend to whom I had been telling many anecdotes that reflected my upbringing suggested that I write a book of short stories. I thought the idea was terrific.

The stories here are not about my family, yet I hope they show about Hutterite life so that the outsider can understand this life-style a bit better. Of course, to say that they are purely fictitious would not be entirely true. I will leave it up to the reader to decide. I should point out that it is not my intention to stereotype my people, even though there are many strong characteristics that people in such a community have in common, and which are apparent in my stories. It is rather my wish to entertain.

I recall a Mennonite writer saying that early Mennonite fiction writers were thought of as "liars and rascals" by their more conservative members, who felt that writing about their life-style was wrong and sinful. I expect, because of the conscious effort to withdraw from the world and the strict and conservative viewpoints held by many Hutterites, the same will possibly be said about my stories. But the words of writer and poet David Waltner-Toews ring true here. In the Summer 1990 issue of *Prairie Fire* was his comment: "In the end, of course, dogmas, no matter how loudly they bark, drown pitifully in the stories of real life, whether biblical, Mennonite, or otherwise. Stories lead one back into the passionate, sad and exhilarating experiences of life and dogmas lead to nowhere but valleys of dry bones."

Samuel Hofer / 1991

MARRYING AWAY

My oldest sister Ida, who's twenty-eight, five years older than me, she doesn't live here any more. The house seemed hollow at first after she married away to another colony, almost as if there was an echo every time somebody moved or spoke. From her first letters, I got the feeling the echo in her house was more like that inside an empty granary. Maybe it would've helped if she hadn't written so clearly because my mother started crying.

Ida, she never had as much free time outside German and English school as most of the girls her age had while growing up, because she was the first in our family. Many many times while her comrades would play hide and seek or dodge-ball, or pick rosehips out in the cow pasture with the boys, Ida would have to stay close to home and take care of me and my brothers and sisters. To pass the time, she was always making up stories in her mind and writing them down, about a girl named Sarah Gross who was her imaginary pen-pal living in far-off Manitoba. This girl — I know because Ida let me read her stories — had a box of fancy perfumes and jewels hidden in a secret compartment inside the walls of their family unit, of which only she knew about. She could wear them to school and right under the German school teacher's nose because they were invisible to everybody but her.

Like Ida, I knew her stories could never

come true in the colony, but I sure enjoyed reading them because they made me feel bold inside. And Ida's stories inspired me to write my own. Mostly I write stories about stuff that happens around here. Hardly anybody outside my family except my girlfriend Kleinsasser Elizabeth knows. You know how people spread stories about such things that are different. Every time a story circulates, it ricochets from one colony to the next, then gets chewed over and over till it's like a legend. I'd rather not stand out that much.

Before Ida married with Martin Entz from Picture Butte colony out in Alberta, they went together for three years. They first met when she was at Green Ridge colony somewhere by Lethbridge, helping her friend Debbie Wurz's family repaint the interior of their house. Ida came home with high spirits, as if she had been to heaven for two weeks.

Me and my brothers teased her about having to come down from the clouds sooner or later, but she didn't come down for a long, long time, probably not till just before she got married. We could see in her eyes that faraway look that showed she was feeling like someone in the very last pages of those Harlequin Romance books, of which she had a whole drawer full. Our cousin Helen Wipf and Judith Waldner from the old Isaac Waldner family, who are a few years older than my sister, passed on their collection of Harlequin Romance books to her when they got baptised. My father burned almost all of them in our ash barrel outside.

"So what's wrong with reading romance books?" Ida complained when Father wasn't around. "Can't a girl do anything other than work all the time?"

"You know these books only keep you from reading the Bible," my mother echoed my father's words. "Worldly books are from the devil; they don't belong to us."

But Ida, she kept reading romance books in privacy anyway. And although she kept it quiet, she practised writing love letters for when she'd have a boyfriend.

"When that boyfriend finally arrives, he'll be so mesmerized by your words, he won't be able to stay away; we might have to chase him off," I teased her one time when she showed me a letter she had written.

Well, she sure got her chance. Hardly a week had gone by after she came back from Green Ridge colony, when the first Thinking of You card arrived with the mail. Ida had a response card and a letter ready which she made sure somebody mailed on the very first trip that went to Moose Jaw.

In two weeks a bigger and more serious card came, with a letter inside. Ida wouldn't let me and my brothers read the letter, but four Sundays hadn't even passed when Martin Entz hitchhiked up here to visit with her. He came walking along the gravel road that leads into our colony from the highway, where someone had dropped him off. He was a big fellow, the kind of guy who could pitch alfalfa bales from the very bottom layer of the haywagon to the top of the haystack without straining himself. Ida sure seemed tiny sitting next to him on a bench. One thing me and my family noticed quick was that Martin had one heck of a nice personality and he was a real sensible guy. Knew a lot about mechanics, he did. And he didn't smoke, drink too much nor act big-shottish in front of the girls.

Also, he had memorized lots of Charlie Pride and Buck Owens songs which he played on John Waldner's guitar. All the boys and girls were gathered in the kindergarten house where young adults gather in the evening when guests come, for some coffee and sweet stuff that the girls bring over. It was pretty obvious what Ida saw in Martin. Before his two-day visit was over, she already acknowledged that she had accepted his proposal for them to go together.

"Boy, do they ever make a nice couple," some of the boys and girls said.

From looking at Ida, the way she had her plump arm wrapped around Martin's shoulder in the little school, we could see that she was very proud of finally having a boyfriend. Her grey-blue eyes were

17

shining like sunlight off the dugout and she beamed happily at everybody. Ida looks much like my girlfriend Kleinsasser Elizabeth, only she's shorter. She has the same colour hair as Elizabeth, which is dark like topsoil after a rain. Ida's face is round and pudgy and it seems like she has a sunburn on her face, but she doesn't. The part of her face and chin that is covered by her kerchief looks pale in comparison. And she's strong. My mother says girls with wide hips like her are good for having lots of children.

Actually, my mother wasn't pleased at first with Ida's boyfriend.

"Why can't you wait for Chris Hofer?" she said. "You wouldn't need to marry away from Old Lakeville and your family."

My mother, she married away from her family and her home colony. I remember one time when I was about six, three colonies from Montana, including Fairfield, my mother's home colony, got a visiting trip going to Old Lakeville and Caronport colony by Moose Jaw. For some dumb reason none of her family could come. I still remember her, bent over at our living-room closet, sobbing and hurting quietly; it took my father a long time to lighten her heart.

But the problem with Chris Hofer was that he was run away. The story was, and had been for a whole year, that he'd be coming back soon. Right after New Year's, his mother said. Then when he didn't show up, she said he had promised to come home right after Easter, then after spring seeding, which got pushed till after harvesting. Ida and Chris had almost started going together before he ran away and got himself a custom combining job out in the world, travelling as far as Kansas down in the States. For two years Ida had kept waiting and waiting, and writing him lots of letters. Once in a while she'd receive a card and a letter from him, which made her happy for a few days. But it didn't take long till the effects of the letter had worn off and she was depressed again.

"Mother, I can't wait forever for Chris," she

said. "I've written all the words in my heart away to him. If he still wants me, when and if he ever comes back, he's gonna be too late."

My girlfriend Kleinsasser Elizabeth said she figured it took a lot of courage for Ida to make a stand like that. When I was run away from Old Lakeville for a year and a half before me and Elizabeth started going together, she had waited patiently for me; she even prayed for me that I wouldn't get involved with an English girl out in the world. I consider myself pretty lucky. But it sure would've been nice to have an English girlfriend for a while anyway, because I was awful lonely out there, away from my family.

On Saturday, the day before Ida's wedding, our whole family drove out to Picture Butte colony. Martin Entz and his brother Matthew and Ida rode ahead in Picture Butte colony's International Loadstar on which we had loaded Ida's personal belongings: her clothing and fabrics, her bedding, her chest of drawers, wedding gifts, her sewing machine and other items. Our family followed behind, packed into the Chevy van. Before we left that morning, all the families from Old Lakeville, from the youngest to the oldest, were gathered on our lawn to say goodbye to Ida.

Some of the girls, especially Katrina Hofer our German school teacher's daughter, were weeping as they hugged my sister for the last time. I felt like pulling out my own handkerchief and letting out my tears, but I didn't.

"I'll write you a letter every week, but I'm sure you will feel at home at Picture Butte before long," Katrina Hofer said, trying to cheer up my sister. At Old Lakeville, the women and the unbaptised girls rotate weeks as the cooks in the community kitchen, and Ida and Katrina Hofer were always a pair.

"And make sure you come to visit as often as you can," my sister said, sponging her eyes with her handkerchief. "You can stay for as long as you like."

"Maybe you could move to Old Lakeville," I joked to Martin Entz. "Ida could stay here then; I'm sure the field boss could find a job for you."

Martin gave a small laugh, but he was biting his lip and his Adam's apple bobbed up and down a few times. It seemed like he was feeling guilty, just standing there beside my sister, watching her cry and not being able to do anything about it.

"Elias, I'd move anywhere if that's what made Ida happy," he said slowly. "If the traditions allowed that."

But these traditions had been frozen for so long, I doubted that anything was about to change in a hurry. I asked my father about this once and he said: "Elias, we have enough friction amongst the men as it is. The cowman wants this in his barn, the carpenter wants that in the shop; it goes on and on. If we had a man marry here from another colony, with different notions on how things are supposed to be done and the power to implement his ideas, we'd be forever arguing."

I thought about that, and I figured Ida would be able to adapt to life at Picture Butte much easier than Martin would to Old Lakeville, because she'd never hold a position of authority like Martin could.

Anyway, we arrived at Picture Butte colony at about half-to-five in the afternoon. Right away people already dressed in their Sunday clothes scurried from every direction and children who had been waiting on the gravel road leading into the colony site started hopping with excitement. The house where we stepped off, which was Martin's parents' unit, was packed like corn on a cob in less than twenty minutes as people tried getting a peek at the bride and groom. Martin's sisters had laid cardboard on the floors of the entire unit to protect the linoleum from all the traffic, and had carried about ten backless benches from the community mess hall and placed them in rows for people to sit on. At about the same time we pulled in, a couple other vans and a crewcab arrived from other colonies; three of Martin's older sisters who had married away came with their husbands and at least fifteen children. Martin's sisters Rachel and Anna opened a few bottles of beer and orange pop and walked around with a tray of glasses.

"Welcome to Picture Butte," they said. Ida just smiled a little and looked about shyly at all the people who had gathered.

"Well, this is your new home," Martin's father said to Ida as he raised a glass of beer to make a toast. "We hope you will enjoy it here."

In the evening after supper and before the shivaree, all the people came together in the Entz family unit and Ida and Martin poured each adult a small shot of apricot brandy mixed with whisky.

"Here's to your health," "Lots of luck," "Welcome to Picture Butte colony," they toasted. And Ida and Martin kept nodding and smiling politely. I've always wondered how a person can do so much smiling in one day, especially when a person moves to a new colony where almost everybody's a stranger at first. I think our * Michael Wipf-vetter from Prairieland colony by Swift Current had a lot to do with keeping Ida smiling, and everybody laughing, period. Only God knows how he got permission to come to the wedding in the first place, because only immediate family members are allowed. But Michael-vetter has his tricks of getting on every wheel that turns. He's a real funny person and he tells jokes all the time. I could see Ida was glad that our fat vetter had come to the wedding.

At about eight o'clock the shivaree got started in the community kitchen, where everybody, young and old, came together to sing. All the tables were pushed to one side and the long wooden benches were placed parallel to each other, covering

---

* *Vetter* (singular) *Vette* (plural) is the Hutterite term for uncle, but the word is also used to show respect (with variation) to all older men.

the entire hall, except for a space in the centre. Ida and Martin sat on chairs that were placed side by side at the far end of the clearing so that they could see all the action. Unlike the seating arrangements at church and at the dinner table, where men sit on one side of the room and women on the other, at a shivaree everybody is free to sit wherever they choose.

At first we sang regular songs like: *Gott Ist Die Liebe* and *Ach, Sohn Du Liebster Herr Jesus Mine*, then a mixture of German and English songs. Gee, those boys and girls from Picture Butte colony knew a lot of hymns and Country and Western songs! And they sure knew how to harmonize! Martin's cousin David Wurz sneaked a guitar into the hall when there were no preachers around and he sang a few Johnny Cash songs and then some Loretta Lynn duets with his sister Christina.

I'm not much of a singer. My voice doesn't have much of a steering wheel, but after I had wet my throat with the two or three Labatt's beers that Matthew Entz kept pushing into my and my brothers' hands, out of hospitality, I was ready to contribute a little. I sang one of my favourite songs of Conway Twitty's, called "It's Only Make Believe," which I had learned from listening to my second cousin Kleinsasser George's tape player he has hidden away in the truck garage at Old Lakeville colony. The beer had washed half the words from my memory, so I sang the same verse three times. Still everybody cheered and clapped as if I was a famous singer. They knew I had a few under the cap, but nobody cared much. I sure didn't. The people from Picture Butte colony got such a kick out of me singing this song — I had to raise my voice to the ceiling at the chorus — they talked Ida and Martin into requesting that I sing it twice, as a special dedication to the bride and groom. So I did. I don't think anybody was listening to the words, they just wanted to hear me sing.

Between group and solo songs, my Michael Wipf-vetter kept nagging Matthew Hofer, who was the chairman, to get people laughing more. He took the floor and cracked jokes and everybody bounced so hard, the benches were sliding a little. Daniel Waldner-vetter the first preacher stuck his head through the doorway once and warned us to keep our laughter under control. But as soon as the preacher was gone, my vetter turned on the volume once again. He didn't seem to care what people thought about him, a forty-year-old fat man, as big as a barn, acting like a young punk.

"This is a shivaree," he said. "And time for some fun." He told some worn-out Ukrainian jokes, only he switched them around.

"How many Dariusleut Hutterites does it take to screw in a light bulb," he quizzed us.

Everybody knew the answer to the Ukrainian joke, but we knew his joke would be different, so everybody called out: "WHAT?"

"You need four people," he said. "Two preachers to give you permission, one boss to give you the light bulb, and one man to screw it in."

The whole crowd exploded from his jokes — some people have the talent of turning even unfunny jokes into good ones — people said later that our laughter could be heard clear across the colony and right down in people's basements. We also heard that the preacher had given my vetter a sharp lecture about all the excess laughter he created.

At one point during the shivaree Michael-vetter jumped up and interrupted the chairman and announced that it was time to sing the traditional Hutterite German tribute and kissing song to the bride and groom, whereby about ten men gathered around Ida and Martin and boomed out the song of good wishes and cheer in loud and boisterous voices. At the end of the song, there was a moment of deliberate silence, so that everybody could hear Ida and Martin smooching like singing sparrows behind the wall of men. The whole crowd cheered some more and then the men disbanded, showing the couple hugging and still kissing each other.

All throughout the shivaree, Ida and Martin held hands and he had one arm around her

23

shoulder; once in a while he whispered something into her ear, probably pointing out who was who amongst the people from Picture Butte colony. Ida was looking around the hall smiling shyly. Ida is much like me; she never was one to make much noise. She'd be happy just to sit unnoticed in a crowd.

"People who aren't shy have it much easier," my mother often says. "Sometimes a person needs a lot of nerves. Otherwise, she can easily become like invisible."

Well, I've got a pretty good notion how my sister felt amongst all these new people from Picture Butte colony, who'd be her new neighbours from now on.

"So do you think you'll like it here?" I asked her later, during the intermission.

She just smiled at me and said quietly. "I guess it's kind of too late to turn back now."

The next morning at the special church service, Ida and Martin stood up in front of the whole community after the service and Daniel-vetter the preacher called them by name to the centre of the room, where he married them together.

Because this was a wedding, the women were allowed to wear their multi-coloured dresses to church. I couldn't take my eyes off them because they all looked so special and distinctive in those flowered dresses of blue, green, gold, yellow, black, orange and almost every other colour you can think of. Ida had on a glossy looking wedding dress with two shades of bold blue carnations on it for a design. Martin had on a regular black Sunday suit and a black clip-on tie and white shirt, which is what most of the men were wearing.

The church house was as still as the inside of a root cellar when Daniel-vetter read the marriage vows from his sermon book and waited for the "yes" answer. Ida's voice, when she spoke for the first time in front of all the people, seemed so weak and shy, almost a whisper, and everybody had to listen real hard to hear her.

After the church service, we had the long long wedding meal of large broiler chickens, noodle soup and gooseberry *moos* in the community mess hall. Somehow my Michael Wipf-vetter got himself assigned to be one of the men who went round to all the tables three times, pouring beer.

"Saufts boys, fressts boys," he said to me and my brothers and Martin's brothers, who were all sitting together at one end of the long table. We just shook our heads and rolled our eyes back and forth. The terms he used, when he said "drink boys, eat boys" in German, means gorging oneself full like an animal would. Lucky there were no preachers within hearing range.

"I think he has a few too many under the cap already," my brother Johann said when my uncle had moved on to another part of the table.

At two in the afternoon, after a break from dinner and after a short shivaree, the bell on top of the community kitchen rang and the *hochzeit* started in the dining hall. The preacher started it off with a special matrimonial song, after which he made a short speech.

"Keep in mind, even though this is a time for merriment," he said. "We ought to be careful and eat and drink like God-fearing Christians."

Then all afternoon we sang *hochzeit lieder*, which everybody was reading out of handwritten and duplicated books, and we drank beer and ate pretzels and peanuts, ice cream and cake. We toasted and made wishes till there wasn't anything left to toast about and we started raising our glasses to the crops that we'd grow, not that summer, but the summer after. I guess a person has only so many things to toast about. I had always wondered how the bride and groom could keep from drinking too much when there are a hundred people constantly coming up to their table, wishing to have a drink with them and bump glasses together. I noticed that Ida, every time she'd lift her glass, would take just a tiny sip, maybe five drops.

At the end of the *hochzeit*, a few of us were walking wobbly already. There were a couple of guys who had drunk too much and had to leave before the closing song. One of them had claimed he couldn't get drunk because he had coated his stomach by drinking a glass of thick cream he had scooped from the top of the milk tank in the dairy barn. Either his method didn't work or he couldn't handle his beer too well. A few of the guys from Picture Butte colony even went to toast with the children, who drank orange and ginger-ale pop.

My voice was still a bit hoarse from all the singing the next day. Monday afternoon, when the dreary time came for me and my family to pack into the van and head back to Old Lakeville colony, without Ida of course, the mood had changed like from day to night. Gone was the laughter, and gone was the singing and the merriment we had enjoyed so much on Sunday, except maybe wherever our Michael Wipf-vetter happened to be. Somebody said that he and Daniel-vetter the preacher had gotten into an argument the evening before about my uncle causing too much laughter at the *hochzeit*.

Ida and our whole family and Martin's family were all crowded into the couple's brand-new unit just minutes before we left Picture Butte. The van was parked outside, all gassed up, and through the half-transparent curtains I could see that at least fifty of Ida's new neighbours had gathered to watch us go. Martin was sitting beside Ida on a leatherette upholstered bench which was a gift Martin's parents had made for them. Martin was holding Ida's hand and looking glumly at the floor. He no longer had his arm around her shoulders like he had all the time during the festivities, as if now that the party was over and life would be getting back to normal, there'd be no need to show as much affection so that everybody could see it.

26

Like Ida, my mother and my other sisters were crying, sometimes shamelessly letting out a burst of emotion, then letting it subside gradually. Even my father, who I hadn't seen crying more than once or twice, had moist eyes.

"Well, what can we do?" he said slowly. "This is how it goes. We know you will take good care of our Ida. We pray she'll be loved by everybody and we know she'll be good for your community."

My father for the most part had been quiet throughout the whole affair. I knew he held back his feelings a lot, like the time when I was ten or twelve, when he cut his thumb with a band saw in the carpentry shop at home. I remembered how he had held out his hand, as helpless as a baby, while my mother poured Zmo on it and wrapped his hand with gauze, fixing it till somebody rushed him to a doctor in Moose Jaw. Although the raw flesh, where the blade had ripped into his thumb and right to the bone, was exposed, he didn't cry. He just gritted his teeth and held the pain inside.

I still remember, as we drove out of Picture Butte colony, looking back till we were at the turnoff past the garages. Ida was still standing outside on the lawn, watching us pull away. Her drenched white handkerchief was still out, which doubtlessly was not the last time she used it in the days following this. Almost everybody from Picture Butte colony had come together and were standing by, watching.

That was two years ago. Last week I drove my mother to Picture Butte colony; she's staying out there for three weeks, taking care of my sister. Ida just had her second child, a little girl, who she named Dorothy, after my mother.

"It was hard being away from my family at first and adjusting to different people," Ida told us. "And it still is sometimes. It's after you're married when it really comes to your head that you're not at home any more.

"When you're far away from your family, knowing you'll never again live in the same colony, all your romantic notions dry up like *räascha zwieback* in the oven. That's when those little things that have always kind of irritated you about your boyfriend but which you chose to ignore before marriage come to haunt you like bad dreams, and you have to pray to God for patience."

We were lunching on coffee and freshly baked *shnecki* in Ida's unit. Martin, he just nodded his head in agreement. But he and Ida were smiling like I remembered them at home when they first started going together. Ida's face is thinner now and not as red as it used to be, and she looks older, more like my mother. And Martin has grown a thick red-brown beard.

"It's much better here now," Ida told me later, her face beaming with pride as she cuddled the little bundle in which Dorothy was wrapped. "I have a family to take care of. And Heaven Father willing, nobody can take them away from me. Me and Martin and Thomas and Dorothy. We're a family."

BORN HUTTERITE

Until I was seven or eight years old, I believed I was delivered from heaven in a cotton pouch via the stork. My parents revealed as much to me and my brothers and sisters — that it was the stork who brought babies to the mothers of Old Lakeville colony, it was the stork who decided how many children there'd be in each family, and it was the stork who decided whether a baby would be a boy or a girl.

Thus, early one Saturday morning, I arrived unannounced, yet welcomed by everyone. A Hutterite baby boy, destined to become another farmer in the tradition of our forbears going back several hundred years.

At age five I was led to believe — when my curious mind probed into grown-ups' affairs too close for their comfort — that my sister Katie could just as well have been my * Martha-pasel's little girl if she hadn't taken careful precautions.

"It wasn't that I didn't want her, Eli," Martha-Pasel explained when I was being nosey. "It was because I already have six boys and eight girls; my house is full."

I couldn't imagine that she'd have shirked her duty as a mother and constant giver of herself,

---

* *Pasle* (singular) *Paslen* (plural) is the Hutterite term for aunt. The term is also used for all older women.

ever. And neither would've my mother. Certainly, there would have been other solutions. As I learned, my pasle's solution was to keep an eye out for the stork day and night and lie low so that when the stork came around he wouldn't find her and he would have to go to someone else's house to deliver the baby. At night she would lock the doors, close the windows, pull down the blinds and stay as quiet as possible.

On the morning of Katie's arrival, she saw the stork coming already from many miles away, only a dot on the western horizon as he flew over Old Wives' Lake. Quickly, she double-checked the secured doors and windows, then hid in her bedroom closet. So the stork descended on our house instead, flew through the wide open window, unrolled his cotton pouch, and dropped Katie at my mother's side, who was lying in bed, contemplating the day and the work ahead of her. Of course, she never got up that morning! The stork walloped her with one of his massive wings to make her sick so she'd have to stay home and take care of Katie for a few weeks. Then he flew back to Heaven Father for another baby to bring to a mother elsewhere, maybe to an English mother out in the world, nobody knew.

It's a good thing we didn't remember much of our first few years of life because if we did, the grown-ups wouldn't have gotten away with this stork story so easily.

Oh, we asked all right. Me and my older brother Tim, my younger brother Johann, and our comrades Kleinsasser George, Kleinsasser Steve and other boys we went to kindergarten with were quite certain that there was something that was being held from us. What brought about this suspicion was Tim's announcement one day that he knew for sure that goslings came from eggs hatched in an incubator. And he also knew where the eggs came from. He had spent time in the goose barn with our Michael Wipf-vetter's boys. Together, they had made these important observations.

But Tim held back bits of information from me and Johann. He was probably embarrassed about the whole thing just like I was when I guessed the truth a couple of years later.

Things like s-e-x and reproduction still aren't talked about in the open here and definitely not in front of children. But the children of today are more aware than me and my brothers and sisters were at their age.

When I was in my third year of English school, Andrew Hofer-vetter the German school teacher of that time censored all the books in our little library in English school, erasing all clues of where exactly we originated from. A new set of World Book encyclopedias was carefully purged of information and photographs on topics such as fertility, pregnancy, and any other s-e-x related articles. Whatever was considered unsuitable for children to know about was cut out or glued shut, which of course was a dead giveaway. Every student that could read English already spent every free moment during the first week that we had these encyclopedias hunting for the clues that had been missed. And the school's twelve-hundred page Webster dictionary proved to be most enlightening.

Like the rest of the boys — girls I don't know about, they may have found out sooner — I caught on eventually with or without encyclopedias. As there were chickens, ducks, geese, cows, pigs, and family upon family of cats on the farm that did strange things, I put one and one together and within a short time was asking these kinds of questions whenever the opportunity arose. No, I never asked directly! I was much too embarrassed about the whole sinful affair to openly talk about it.

"Anybody who asks too many questions won't live long," my mother said. "Someone with too much knowledge could become harmful to the colony."

"You don't need to know so many things," was my father's advice. "The more you know, the more questions you have. People who know much, end up thinking they're better than their neighbours. And before long they're vain and start having vast differences like people out in the world. That's sinning against Heaven Father."

Hofer David-vetter our German school teacher reinforced my parents' words of wisdom.

"What you need to concern yourself with is not what the world is doing, but rather what Heaven Father wants us to do right here in the colony. Be thankful that you were not born out there, where free will, which leads to sin, is rampant. You are oh so fortunate not having been born out there, and even though the world children have all their toys and all their fancy clothes and don't have to memorize German verses every day like you do, what good will it be for them at the end of the world?"

I suppose because of my will to live beyond childhood age, my parents' and our German school teacher's advice was one of my earliest lessons in economy and simplicity. I'm just twenty-three years old and am far from knowing everything there is to know about our religion.

"Being born a Hutterite is just the beginning. After you've had a number of years of communal life training behind you, that's when you'll know. It's after you're baptised, after you've been enlightened by many years of going to church, reading the Bible and praying for strength, that's when you'll understand, I mean really understand, why you were born a Hutterite," my father says. And in the same breath he warns me, like he does often, that I should ease off on reading worldly books. I borrow a few now and then from the public library in Moose Jaw, to read in my spare time.

The other day my Paul Paul-vetter's Ronnie, who's only six years old, was playing at our house with some of his boy and girl comrades.

"My mamma says the stork will soon bring our family another baby," he said. "She wrote him a letter and she says to him we want another girl."

One of the children, who's older than Ronnie, grinned slyly at me.

"Oh yes, I've seen the stork," I said, looking up from the book I was reading. "He has these huge wings, and he flies directly from heaven...."

FEEL GOOD TEA

Except for the crazy stories that still go around
outside our colony and come up once in a while five
years later and shame my father and mother,
everybody here has forgiven — and almost forgotten
— what happened. But I tell you, the first time my
brother Tim came home for a visit from his job up
north by Leduc, near Edmonton, after his sudden
departure, he came late, after the sun had taken its
light to the other side of the pasture hills. He
crawled slowly into Old Lakeville colony with his
headlights off and he parked his 1976 Mercury
Bobcat away from sight behind our tractor garage.

"You're the one who made the bed, you sleep
in it," my mother said to him. He was sitting at our
living-room table, beer in hand, smoking a cigarette
in front of our whole family. Even in front of all the
other people who had quickly gathered in our house.
He's been smoking since long before he left Old
Lakeville, only now he smokes without guilt. His
English clothes made him stand out like one white
goose in a flock of grey ones.

When Kleinsasser Abe-vetter our first
preacher came by, Tim did put away his cigarette,
mind you. My mother pleaded with him that he
ought to have at least that much respect, especially
after the commotion he caused before he ran away.
Abe-vetter walked silently into the room, which had
become as still as the inside of the root cellar. His

dark eyes were sterner than ever as he contemplated my brother's western-type shirt and blue jeans. Kleinsasser Abe-vetter is around fifty-five years old, and he's short and heavy, but not fat. His black beard is always trimmed real tidy, and his pants, which he has pulled a few inches above his waist with his suspenders, make his legs appear longer than they really are. I figure he'd already been in bed because his pyjamas were sticking out at the arm cuffs of his black jacket. From the sudden stillness and everybody shifting eyes back and forth from Tim to our preacher, I figured everybody was getting ready to listen to a lecture that had been brewing in Kleinsasser Abe-vetter's mind for a long time.

"Just look at you, Wipf Timotheas," he began, "Now that you are outside in that stinking world; a world that always beckons its evil ways to us. Can you see a fruitful outcome out there?" Tim just cast his eyes to the floor, then rolled them back and forth from his cowboy boots to a spot underneath the table. His fingers were busy, clawing at the label on his Labatt's beer bottle.

"A real fool you made of us, Timotheas. The shame and the agony you brought upon us through your flirtation with that lust of the flesh that you from young on have been taught to refrain from. Have you no afterthought about this?"

When Abe-vetter lectures, he asks questions, but we figured out long ago, the way to cut a lecture short is to stay quiet and let him talk. Tim just kept staring down as if his gaze was welded to the floor.

Hofer Barbara and her husband Hofer David our garden man were some of the other people who came huffing over to our unit as soon as the word went round that my brother had shown up.

"If that Wipf Tim ever comes home to visit, he'll hear from me, that...that...I might even dare talk him on rude," Hofer Barbara had said when the news went round of Tim's fast exodus from Old Lakeville. Both of them are quite fat, so it's hard to miss them when they walk into a room. When they squeezed in, everybody had to move their chairs back some. Even a bench had to be moved closer to the wall.

"You foolish *towga nixer*," she said, waving her finger at my brother. "When you left, I could have strapped you hard enough to make the red soup squirt!"

Hofer David's waving finger wasn't far behind his wife's. His attention was directed at Katrina Hofer, their daughter, who was sitting beside my brother.

"Katrina, let yourself be warned. From him you hold yourself away. He will corrupt you to that stinking world which he ran off to if you don't watch out."

Katrina Hofer and Tim, though they weren't really going together, were going on dates once in a while before he ran away. Me and my brothers and sisters always figured that the two would go together. Katrina wanted that very much, but Tim used to say, "I'm not ready to get tied to nobody."

"Father!" Katrina said, coming to Tim's defence. "That was ten months ago. Can't anybody forget about this already?" She had been inching her chair closer to my brother's.

"FORGET?" about ten voices chorused.

I had seen in the beginning already — unlike when Kleinsasser Abe-vetter lectured him — when Hofer Barbara had started waving her finger at my brother that he was grinning behind his hand, with which he was pretending to rub his forehead. His Cargill cap he had pulled down almost to his eyebrows and his long hair was sticking out the sides like straw. Tim is tall and skinny. When he walks it looks like he's carrying a bag of flour on his back and his face is so red, you'd think he was straining himself. His eyes are big and light blue and he has a few milky hairs for a moustache and milky hairs for side-beards.

Actually, Tim had run away — tried running away that is — from Old Lakeville colony once before, when he was only sixteen. My father, when he found out, took after him that day and found him at the River Street Pool Hall in Moose Jaw. Tim already had on the English clothes he had bought at the Salvation Army. His black clothes he had chucked in the Laidlaw disposal bin behind the Chop Suey restaurant. Boy, we laughed when he came home, his clothes reeking of ketchup, pickles and soya sauce.

My brother is the type of guy who dreams a lot. Since we were kids he's had this dream of making piles of money.

"If I was out in the world," he used to say, "I'd have money like crazy."

Even though it's forbidden to make money for one's own pocket, me and the boys secretly trap coyotes and foxes every fall and winter and work out for our English neighbours once in a while.

At trapping time in the fall, Tim claimed he never had much luck. Maybe he would've had more if he had set his traps further away like most guys did. He wouldn't run further than one mile, just to the far end of the cow pasture. To make things worse, the prices for furs had dropped down to a mere twenty or thirty dollars a pelt. A few years before, the older guys who were now already baptised were getting over three hundred and eighty bucks for one coyote, and over two hundred for a fox.

I think of all the frustrations with trapping, that time Tim caught a badger and got only one dollar for it was the worst. He had spent about six hours scraping the fat in the evening after work, as well as paying my brother Albert five bucks for helping him. I wish I would've had a camera that day when we got our cheques in the mail from the Hudson's Bay fur auction in Montreal. That season Tim had two coyotes, three foxes and one badger. He wasn't paid much for his coyotes and foxes, but the badger upset him the most.

"One lousy dollar for a darn badger," he bellowed, holding up the printout.

"That sucker, he could've bit off my thumb," he had said the day he caught him. He had come home, his face all pale and his handkerchief bound around his thumb which was dripping blood.

Badgers are real tough to kill. The badger had nipped his thumb when Tim tried to dead-choke him, something you never do with a badger because they're as stiff as a pig.

I suppose I had stopped taking Tim's dream seriously about the big money that never showed up. That he would run away to the world eventually I could've believed, even after the shock of Zack Hofer losing his life on the job outside the colony a year earlier. When that happened, Zack's brother Isaac, who had run away at the same time his brother did, immediately quit his job, sold his fancy Camaro and took the first Greyhound bus home. And two other guys from Prairieland colony by Swift Current also came back within a week, that's how shocked they were. But I would never have thought that Tim would go as far as growing dope.

"Just hold your gol darn mouth closed. You know some people would do anything to bugger something up," Tim said, as he showed me the seeds one day when we were alone in our room. "There're enough seeds here to grow three grand worth marijuana. That's what the guy at the pool hall says."

"Where you gonna grow them?" I asked.

"The guy says to grow them where it's dry and hot, up in the pasture somewhere. I'll find a place where the cows can't get to."

"What if someone found it?"

"So?"

"Well, you'd be in trouble, not just ordinary trouble."

"Ah, shoot, it probably looks like any other cottonpickin weed."

"What about neighbours — police?"

Tim shrivelled up his nose and waved his hand. "How often have you seen people walking around on our pasture?"

"That's not the point. Why don't you just run away for a while, if you need money?" I said. "Raising dope! For Pete's sake, nobody does that."

"That's because you guys don't realize there are easier ways of making money than trapping and pitching bales."

"Well, I sure wouldn't raise dope," I argued. "I'd sooner run away for a while. You know, not everybody that runs away gets killed. Zack Hofer, he always was a reckless driver."

"It could happen."

"It could happen anywhere. It could happen tomorrow, driving down the road."

"You're telling me I should run away?" Tim said, squinting his eyes.

"No. Just sooner than raising dope."

Tim looked at me as if he was sorry he had me for a brother or something. "Ah, for cripessake, Elias, stop being so gol darn religious," he said.

Like he explained was best, Tim found a dry and sandy spot just outside the far edge of our pasture, about five kilometres from home. Actually, it wasn't sandy at first, but he sneaked the loader up to the pasture one day and dumped a couple loads of sand on the spot. He sowed his crop on a steep slope of a dried-out ravine.

"Rain won't get a chance to soak in," he told me. He gathered some kochia weed and Canadian thistle seeds and scattered them about, around and in between his crop.

"Once these weeds grow, nobody'll see the difference," he said.

I didn't find out how Tim's crop got mixed up with the colony's peppermint tea when time came to harvest it, till later, after he had run away and was working on a dairy farm up by Yorkton somewhere.

When it happened, me and some of the boys and girls were up at Cypressville colony by Medicine Hat for two weeks helping remodel houses. The day before we came home the story already had reached Cypressville that people from Old Lakeville had been drinking dope. Many of us laughed at this, thinking it was just another rumour going around that some loose wit had started. There are people that do that. But right away my mind jumped on Tim and his marijuana crop.

The moment I walked in the door when we got home my mother and father started shooting questions and demanding explanations, right there and then. Not the next day and no waiting for Judgement Day either.

"Elias, what the demon do you think you're doing, raising dope?" my father fired at me. "Have you no brain left in your head?"

I'd been driving the crewcab for a few hours and was tired and cranky.

"What?" I shot back. "Me! Dope! Hey, don't jump on me with this!"

"Now don't act as if you didn't know anything about it," my mother said. She was waving her finger in front of my nose and my father's finger wasn't far behind hers. One thing about my parents, they sure jump to conclusions real quick. No wonder they have high blood pressure.

"Where's Tim?" I asked, sitting down.

"He ran away," my mother said, and tears started to run down her cheeks.

"What did he say about me?" I asked.

"He left a few words on a piece of paper; he said you could explain." my mother sobbed.

"Only God knows why your brother would do such a thing, but I think he mixed his dope with the peppermint tea from the garden," said my father.

"The people, they drank the tea already," my mother said in turn. "In the hospital we had to take some. The doctor says it's illegal dope, marionna and hashi."

"Marijuana, you mean. Who drank it?" I asked.

"Hofer Barbara and her whole family. Even Abe-vetter. Before church on Sunday they drank it yet."

My stomach suddenly felt heavy and my feet felt wobbly.

"But, didn't anybody notice the difference in the tea?" I asked, sitting down.

41

"Not every family got dope mixed in theirs. We didn't in ours," my mother said. "Hofer Barbara came by our house one day and said that a few seeds of another kind of tea must've got mixed with the peppermint seeds when they planted it, and this year it started growing. That's what Hofer David had said. This new tea would be very strong and make a person feel real good. Some of the ladies had been drinking it before church in the evening and they were amazed at how much easier it was to endure the fifteen minutes of kneeling on the hard floor during the prayer."

I figure Hofer Barbara has been a tea drinker all her life. She's the one who convinced Hofer David to grow camomile and peppermint in the garden when he got the job of garden man. "There is hardly a headache that camomile tea won't cure," she used to say when picking the camomile flowers on her little patch. The women at Sunnyside colony by Havre down in Montana, where she's from, always grew camomile in their flower gardens.

When Hofer Barbara walks into a room, you know she's arrived. She talks and talks. People call her the story woman. I wouldn't be afraid to bet she knows everybody's names in ten colonies, even those who died twenty years ago.

"Your mother could write a book about every family's tree," I said to Isaac Hofer once. "And she could probably even record from those dead already, who had been a good person and who hadn't been, and whether they'd be in heaven or in hell."

"We could see already during the singing at church that there was something wrong with Abe-vetter," my mother said. "People said that he drank three cups of the tea before church to soothe his knees."

"You mean he wasn't wearing his normal scowl?" I asked, trying to make a joke.

"That's nothing to laugh about," my mother said sternly. "Good thing he had a light sermon. You know how he preaches."

Did I know! When Kleinsasser Abe-vetter lets loose a sermon, a person can still hear his voice boom in the ears three hours later.

My sister Frieda and my brother Johann came into the room just then. From the grins on their faces I could see they thought this was funny.

"And when he stood up to preach, he must've thought we were still singing, so he started singing his sermon," Frieda said, holding her sides.

My mind is sharp sometimes and I can easily fill in stuff in my imagination. I'm probably stretching it a just bit in my head, but I could see Kleinsasser Abe-vetter standing up at the desk in front of all the people and thundering out the sermon like an opera singer I had once seen on TV at the Co-op store in Moose Jaw. His voice, I imagined, would be echoing off the walls and rumbling into everybody's aching ears.

"His arm he waved about, pointing at words in his sermon book," Johann joined in. "And then he starts whacking and thumping his book on his palms and flapping it back and forth in circles. With his free hand he's made a fist, which he bangs on the desk, and the song book and Andrew-vetter's glasses lying on it jump up a few inches. Elias, you have no idea of how surprised we are when he puts on this show...just like those preachers on TV out in the world."

"Didn't anybody try calming him down when they saw what was going on?" I asked. "What about Andrew-vetter, didn't he say something?" Andrew Hofer-vetter is our second preacher. The two preachers take turns delivering the sermon. The one not doing the sermon sits nearby, close to the song book, and he leads the singing before and after the sermon.

"Well, Andrew-vetter, he tries, but Abe-vetter yanks his arm loose from him and starts walking up the aisle," Johann said, slapping his knee. "Then he does something really funny. He stops and ruffles some of the little boys' neatly combed hair, pulls their noses and sticks out his thumb through his fingers and pretends he has their noses pulled off. Then you know what happens? Hofer Barbara and Hofer David and Paul Paul-vetter and his wife and

43

a few others join in, singing along with Abe-vetter."

"All we could do was shake our heads," Frieda cut in. "Some of the people left sitting started grumbling."

"Then what happened?" I asked. I figured right about then someone would have had to answer a few questions, real quick.

"People looked Hofer David sharply in the face outside," Frieda said. "I tell you, that poor man was in shock. 'Don't look at me,' he pleaded, 'I didn't give you any dope tea. Think I'm crazy?'"

When I finally got the number for the dairy farm where Tim was working, I called him from a pay-phone in Moose Jaw. The woman who answered said to wait one minute, she'd get him for me. His voice came over the line sounding as if he was cringing, maybe expecting a lecture.

"How'd you get my number?" he asked.

"The Labour Pool gave it to me."

"So, everybody's mad with me, I bet?" he said.

"Well, what you think? What got into your head anyway, mixing your stuff with the tea from the garden? I thought you wanted to sell it."

"Elias, I didn't do that on purpose."

"Not on purpose!" I yelled into the phone. I noticed my brother's voice was starting to waver as if he was on the verge of crying.

"Elias, cripes, you gotta believe me, it was an accident. I was bringing it home to dry underneath the bed — had it packed in plastic bags. On the way home I was walking through the slaughter house where the girls were packing garden stuff and I heard the garden tractor drive up just as I was walking through. I didn't think they'd be working that late and I figured they'd be suspicious if they saw me coming out of the slaughter house carrying away plastic bags stuffed full of something. So I panicked and hid my bags under a table and jumped out the window."

"And they found it?"

"I guess so. The girls were picking camomile and peppermint that evening and they were dividing it up for each family. You know how they throw the whole trailerload on a pile and mix it all together. When I went back later, the girls had already cleaned up the place and my bags were gone."

So there! Every time something different or strange happens at Old Lakeville, the stories go out and circulate and brew for a while amongst the other colonies and even outside. What really expands my gall bladder is that some people are always ready to stretch the story way out of proportion. The way I wrote it was how it happened. Well, I'm not saying I didn't stretch it a little, but cripes, all those other stories, especially the one about us marching down Main Street in Moose Jaw, higher than a kite...well, that's plain crazy.

CARRIE

I can still remember the cold day in October when Peter Waldner from the old Isaac Waldner family ran away and joined the outside world, as many guys do for a while at one time or other. I remember his mother, Katrina Waldner, walking all around Old Lakeville colony and peering into the shops and garages, asking everybody she saw: "Have you seen my Peter anywhere?"

I can also imagine everybody's shock when the news came a few years later that Peter was to get married with a girl from out in the world.

"Peter was a reliable boy," my father said. "Maybe a little too rough with the tractors and with his language, but he was a guy who could pretty near fix anything that needed fixing around the farm. And he wasn't just good with mechanics and stuff; he was one heck of a smart kid to boot. Understood everything the first time around, you didn't have to repeat nothing for him. Too bad he ended up where he is. Jeez, I could cry for him."

I like Peter; he's one heck of a nice guy and me and him are pretty good friends. He's for sure not like most guys from the colony when it comes to doing something different. That guy will try anything at least once, even if it's the craziest thing a guy could do. His round glasses make him look like a person who's been to university. When he was going to English school all the kids at Old Lakeville gave him the nickname of Professor because he spent so much time reading the encyclopedias, and he'd do all kinds of experimenting with science projects. I still remember the Saturday afternoon when everybody at Old Lakeville got a shock of which we talk about to this day every time Peter's name comes up. He blew apart a barrel full of dead broilers behind the chicken barns with some explosives he had made. He had found a half-full box of shotgun bullets in a creek behind the cow pasture that some duck hunters had lost, and he made some dynamite out of fertilizer, diesel fuel and the gunpowder from the bullets. He sure got a mean strapping from Andrew Hofer who was our German school teacher at the time. Fortunately there were no young laying chickens in the laying barn at the time, and most of the broilers in the broiler barn had already been butchered off, because they'd have all piled like they do when they get spooked, and Old Lakeville colony could've lost half the flock.

"It's too late for him now! Now his eyes will open, but he can't very easily come back anymore," people said when the word came out about his marriage. "He's gotta stay out in that stinking world for good now, God have mercy on his poor soul."

People here never divorce, so the thought that somebody who's lived in the colony would get divorced is as rare as orange trees growing in southern Saskatchewan. The only way a runaway person could come back to live in the colony after marrying outside would be if the spouse died or ran off or came back and converted to Hutterite traditions and religion.

When Peter got married I was out in the world myself; I was run away from Old Lakeville colony just for a year and a half. At the time, I was working on a dairy farm by Rosthern north of Saskatoon. Once in a while, usually on Saturday nights, I'd go into the city and me and Peter would have ourselves a few beers in the Texas T or Max's Diner with his English girl named Carrie, the girl he got married with.

Like I said, Peter doesn't fool around. He has his very own business these days, up near Robin

Hood Multifoods where Old Lakeville buys flour, which he named Carrie's Printing. When he came to Saskatoon after a couple of years on a pig farm up by North Battleford he got himself a job in a printing outfit in Saskatoon called Idylwyld Printing. In the first month his boss had him walking around to all the businesses and selling custom-printed Christmas cards.

"I'm a damn good salesman, Elias," he said to me when I first connected up with him and me and him and his girl Carrie were having coffee in Max's Diner. "After Christmas, my boss, he wanted to hire me to be his regular salesman."

"And you took the job?" I asked, leaning forward across the table.

"Well, not really," he said, his fingers tapping on the table to the beat of the loud music that was playing. "After two months of knocking on doors, being polite and smiling at everybody, I wanted to leave and get me another job. The kind on which I wouldn't have to wear a damn tie. So after Christmas, I started looking around, and I was quite shocked at the few jobs available that would hire someone with just grade eight. I mean, if you don't got at least grade ten and you want to make more than five bucks an hour here in the city, you ain't gonna get too far. If ever I've seen something ridiculous it's those jobs posted at the Canada Labour Office for which you gotta be on welfare to get hired, and then they don't pay you no more than what you'd get from welfare in the first place. Well, I wasn't interested in going back to feeding pigs and shovelling manure. I wanted to live close to the action, so I settled for a five dollar an hour job working for a pizza place up on Eighth Street. That's where I met Carrie."

He winked at Carrie, who had her skinny arm wrapped around his shoulder and was stroking his long sidebeard. He hugged her against his shoulder and she reached up her head to kiss his lips, then they rubbed noses together with their eyes closed and Peter murmured and laughed softly from deep in his throat. It seemed to me he loved her very much and I suddenly felt homesick and wished I could be with Kleinsasser Elizabeth, with who I had almost started going together before I left home. I looked away, embarrassed, and my eyes roamed the restaurant, momentarily stopping now and again to focus on people deep in conversation.

"Anyway, I went back to Idylwyld Printing after a while because I realized I wasn't getting anywhere working for minimum wage," Peter continued when he finally looked up. "I talked my boss into letting me run the press a little. I'm glad to say they're paying me eight bucks an hour now, running the press forty hours every week. That's how damn good a printer I am. Running those presses is easier'n hell, I'm gonna save up a few bucks and buy my own press; already got one lined up. I figure if I work like crazy, we can print up enough flyers and business cards and letterheads to make a hell of a lot of money. Me and Carrie, we'll be partners and we're gonna start out in our basement suite, so we don't have much overhead. Ain't that right, sweetie?"

Carrie cleared her throat and took a long swallow of coffee, then looked across the table at me and smiled, showing her beautiful teeth.

"He's got plans alright," she said. All this time while Peter was talking, Carrie had nodded to every word Peter had said. I got the feeling she was quite attached to him.

"Yeah, Elias, you gotta have a plan if you're gonna get anywhere these days," Peter went right on. "You gotta think big. You can't be working for someone else forever. Sooner or later you gotta strike it out on your own if you want to get ahead. They taught me how to work damn hard at home and I gotta prove there ain't nothing nor nobody that's gonna stop me."

There was a lapse in our conversation. All of us were deep in thought; I noticed that Carrie's smile melted away when Peter said "home". Her arm had never left Peter's shoulder; in fact she had been hanging on to him all evening. She was quite pretty and had hair the colour of corn silk. She wasn't as pretty as Kleinsasser Elizabeth mind you, even with her painted eyelids and her tomato-red lips.

Peter stared into his coffee and pulled and scratched on the paper napkin between his fingers, then raised his head and looked owl-like at me. He took a deep breath and squinted his eyes. His lips curled down slightly.

"Eli, you know what my father says to me when I wrote home explaining that I had found myself a girlfriend and was planning to marry with her?"

"What?"

"He writes me back and says that if get married out in the world, I'm no longer welcome in his house. He says I'd no longer be his son, so there'd be no use coming to visit no more."

"Ah, come on, Pete, he's just saying that; he doesn't really mean it, do you think...?"

"Oh yes he means it! You don't know my father like I do. It's a good thing he never got the job of preacher. You think Abe Kleinsasser is strict, but my father...he gave me and my brothers strappings till I was seventeen till one day my brother Mike tore loose that friggin strap of his and threw it out the window — that's how come we had that broken window, you remember that don't you? 'Don't you ever hit me again if you know what's good for you,' Mike yelled so loud that Aunt Sarah came running from three units away. 'What'er you gonna do?' my father says, his face all paled up. 'Just don't do it, if you don't wanna find out,' my brother said."

I had been watching Carrie dump three teaspoons of sugar into her coffee and stirring it swiftly. Her hand was trembling, a tear was running down her cheek and she started biting her lip real bad. Peter put his arm around his girl's shoulder.

"It's okay, sweetheart," he said softly. "To heck with everybody. See if we give a damn. We'll get married and maybe start a family with or without nobody's blessing."

Peter phoned me up one time, three months after he

and Carrie got married.

"Hey Eli, long time no see," he said. "You stuck out on that bloody dairy farm all the time or what? I ain't heard from you in a month. You got yourself a girl out there so you ain't coming to town no more?"

"Yeah sure," I said. "I wish. There's nothing but cows around here."

The truth was, I had been trying hard to meet English girls from the city. I hadn't felt like hanging around a newly married couple too much because I figured they'd need their privacy, so I'd gone out by myself to try my luck.

Before, I had depended on Peter, who never had any problems talking to English girls. He had no problems getting ourselves introduced real quick to a bunch of people in the Texas T. But he'd always do most of the talking. So I just couldn't get myself to talk to anybody, and after a couple times of just sitting alone at a table in the corner, quietly getting drunk, staring at people partying and dancing to Country and Western music and wishing I had a girlfriend, I gave up on the bar.

I went to the public library in Saskatoon and found a book called "How To Pick Up Girls", written by a fellow named Eric Weber down in the States who claimed his methods worked real good. After a week I got enough nerve together to ask a pretty girl working at the counter of a Kentucky Fried Chicken store for a date. To my amazement, smiling real nice and saying "hi" worked and she smiled back at me. A week later, on another day off, I went back to the same store and said "hi" again. When she said "hi" back, I figured she really liked me and this was the time to pop the big question. Luckily, there were no other people in the store. To my delight, she blushed and agreed on going out on a date with me and I walked out of that place suddenly feeling pretty confident about myself. I punched the air with great satisfaction when I got back to my old Datsun truck and I figured for sure it wouldn't be long now before I'd have myself an English girlfriend. Already in my mind I saw myself driving around Saskatoon with her and going to parties, maybe even going to bed with her because I figured with girls out in the world, that's the first thing that happens. I thought about Kleinsasser Elizabeth just for a minute but quickly pushed her from my mind.

Ten minutes later, after I had stopped shaking and my face had turned back to its natural colour I realized I hadn't even asked the girl for her name nor her phone number. I felt real stupid going back for some more coleslaw and waiting at the counter till there wasn't anybody in the store.

"Where are you from?" she said, giving me a look as if she'd just opened a box of rotten chicken. That's all she said, as if that was all that mattered.

I didn't want to tell her right away that I'm from a dairy farm and that I grew up on a Hutterite colony, just in case she was the type of girl who didn't like farm guys and wouldn't go out with me once she found out who I really was.

"I'm from out by Rosthern," I said.

"Are you French? German?" she asked.

"No. Why?"

"Well, You have an accent."

"Really?" I said. "I didn't know that."

I couldn't figure out why she refused to give me her phone number, but I read in my guide book on how to pick up girls that a guy needs to be persistent. It took three visits to Saskatoon and five orders of Kentucky Fried Chicken in the evening after milking the cows before I got lucky and chanced upon her shift. By then I had a crop of acne on my face which I had tried clearing up with Clearasil; I've always had trouble with zits when I eat too much fried food. She gave me a phone number this time — for an electrical supply store. Embarrassed like crazy, after making a fool out of myself talking to the girl who answered the phone and kept on insisting that there was nobody with the name Nancy at that place, I retreated back to the farm the next two weekends to nurse my wounded ego.

Anyway, after having gone through all that

I was glad to hear from Peter Waldner.

"Hey, Pete. What's happening?" I said.

"Well, Eli, me and Carrie, we've been thinking about a lot of things these days and last week we said to ourselves that it ain't fair that we can't go see my family on account of my father's thick head. Like, if a person ain't got his family, then what the hell has he got?"

"So you're going home for a visit?" I asked.

"Well yeah. I decided it's worth giving it a shot. I'm wondering if maybe you'd like to come along?"

"What if your father locks you out of the house?"

"Eli, I don't give a hoot. I mean, if he wants to do that, then for cripesake, there ain't nothing I can do about it. I'm hoping Mother is gonna talk him out of it. You know how it is with women. They've got what it takes to soften even the most stubborn man's heart."

From the feelings I had had lately, I knew that what Peter was talking about was true, because I had sure spent many hours in the last two months feeling blue and missing my family.

Nobody spoke much at first as we headed south along the Number Eleven highway headed towards Moose Jaw on the first Saturday I had off. Peter was driving his Ford half-ton and he was playing a tape of a band called Mister Mister on his Alpine stereo. In the back, behind the seat, bottles rattled when we went over a bump on the road.

"I bought a couple cases of beer," Peter said. "And a forty of rye for my father and a new frying pan for my mother. I'm gonna give it to them regardless, even if my father disowns me. Just to show them I ain't turned my back on them because I got married out here."

I looked at Carrie and she smiled at me. I thought she looked extremely pretty, even prettier than Kleinsasser Elizabeth. I really liked her blue-green eyes, and even though her face was too thin and she had a nose that was turned upward just a little, when I looked at her closely I thought she

54

could very easily be the prettiest girl I had ever seen. Maybe it was her neon ski jacket that made her look that pretty, because the pink on it was almost the same colour as her lips and her triangle-shaped earrings. I figured she was maybe about twenty-two years old. Her shyness in front of me had left completely and I wasn't as shy in front of her as I had been when Peter first introduced her to me. I thought to myself, if I could find an English girl like Carrie I'd be real proud.

Carrie put her hand to her side and it brushed against mine. I didn't pull my hand away. That was the first time I had ever touched an English girl and I felt warm all over. I suddenly felt much better about what had happened in the Kentucky Fried Chicken store as my mind played back the whole experience. Maybe I'll quit my job on the dairy farm and get a job in a pizza place, I thought to myself.

My thoughts were interrupted when I realized that Carrie was squeezing my hand.

"You're a nice guy, Elias." she said. I blushed and felt like reaching over and hugging her. It would be so nice, I thought, to actually hug an English girl — any English girl. It wouldn't even matter if she was fat, which Carrie sure wasn't.

"I just hope you don't get chased off the colony," I said. "You gotta understand our folks; they haven't got anything against you personally, it's just that they're old-fashioned and it's not often that a guy who came from the colony gets married with a girl from out here."

"Carrie knows all about that, Elias," Peter said. "I've explained it all to her." He took one hand off the steering wheel and put his arm around her shoulder. "She found the letters my parents wrote. I had intended to burn them, but she found them before I got around to it. That was almost enough for us to break up before we married."

"Well, can you imagine how awful I felt when I read them?" Carrie said. "Letters that called me an evil world person, from whom Peter should stay away, and fall down on his knees day and night to pray for forgiveness and strength, so that God would help him through his deviation from the path so that he could come back to live in the colony."

"They really wrote that?" I asked.

"Yeah, I told you, Eli," Peter said. "My parents are as pious as they come."

"You're a brave person," I said to Carrie. "You really...I mean, you really are brave to come and visit Peter's family." I felt like giving her all kinds of compliments and telling her how pretty she looked; I felt like hugging her, squeezing her and crying with her. But I held back. She must have sensed my feelings because she squeezed my hand with both of hers and smiled at me for a long time, and I felt lucky and confident because I knew her, even though she was married and belonged to my friend Peter Waldner.

The good feeling in my heart was still with me when we pulled into Moose Jaw. Then, as I looked at familiar stores like Army and Navy and The Readers' Bookshop passing by as we cruised down Main Street and thought about my family and the people from Old Lakeville colony, a different feeling came over me. Suddenly the clothes that I was wearing — blue jeans, the shirt with a long collar, my bright red jacket with the letter C on the front and the Cargill cap — made me feel like I was soon to enter into a familiar place as a stranger.

From Peter's actions of chewing frantically on his gum and staring straight ahead without smiling, I figured he too felt like I did, only he had one arm around his wife's shoulder, and she was resting her head against his shoulder.

Nobody spoke much during the half hour it took to travel out to Old Lakeville colony, and when we turned off the highway onto the gravel road leading into the colony, Peter let out a long sigh and said: "Well, here we are. It's too late to turn back now."

I saw my brother Johann on his way back from the hog barn as we drove past the tractor garage. He waved when he recognized me and quickened his step.

We pulled up behind Peter's family's unit of the longhouse and we could see the curtains inside the house stir, blinds go up and polka-dotted heads appear behind the windows, trying to determine who had just pulled up.

"I'll get out here, Pete," I said. "If they won't have you, you can come to my family's house."

I decided to follow Peter and Carrie into the house while waiting for my brother. I was curious to see the reaction Peter's parents would have to Carrie.

As we neared the steps, the door opened slowly and old Isaac Waldner stepped into the doorway. All three of us stopped on the stairs. Isaac raised his hand to his beard and stroked it; I could see that he was in deep thought. And I noticed his eyes were not on Peter, nor on me, but on Carrie. He stood silently for a few seconds, looking at his daughter-in-law, as if trying hard to comprehend her. Finally he spoke.

"So, that's her?" he said in Hutterite German, addressing Peter.

"Yes Dad, and Mom, you too, everybody, this is my wife Carrie."

Everybody nodded shyly to Carrie and old Katrina Waldner extended her hand.

"Well, come on in, it's cold out there, we'll have a cup of coffee and some buns and pork sausages," she said, slowly nodding her head a few times, while a warm smile formed on her face in the same way. But not before — I was watching carefully — she had given old Isaac Waldner an icy stare, which looked like a warning.

As I turned to follow my brother Johann, who had just come up behind me, to my family's house, I saw Peter raising his hand to brush the gloss from his eyes before it had a chance to roll down his face. With his right arm he pulled Carrie close to him as old Katrina Waldner held Carrie's hand in both of hers. And when she reached out and kissed her daughter-in-law on the cheek, I felt like we were floating on a cloud that had broken away from a storm.

ABOUT KINDERGARTEN, GEESE, COYOTES AND TRACTORS AND STUFF.

When the endless chattering sound of our fattening geese drift through my open bedroom window on late summer nights, and when the howls of coyotes beyond the horse creek rouse goose bumps on my back, I find myself reminiscing back to when I was growing up. And I remember about kindergarten and about geese and coyotes and tractors and slingshots and potato shooters.

As is tradition here at Old Lakeville colony, I went to kindergarten from ages three to six. Every morning at eight, the silver-coloured bell on the roof-peak of the community kitchen tolled, and from all four blue and white longhouses kids ambled along the boardwalks to the little school building with the white picket fence around it.

Oh, I remember the odd morning when I or my brothers and sisters tried anchoring ourselves to the ground, door frame or anything else in our path, and insisted on staying at home with Mother. But Mother, she had work to do in the kitchen, garden or slaughter house with the rest of the women. When she or our baby-sitter gripped our arms, there wasn't much we could do except wail and follow. They always knew when we were feigning illness or when it was for real. Not that they didn't care, mind you. They just didn't want us to miss school without having a good reason. Once inside the little school house though, we would surrender to the collective group of children in little school. One of our * little school-ankelen, who rotated days taking care of us, usually got there before we did. And for the most part, all three of them were loyal to the strap.

A short prayer before breakfast was first on the daily agenda. Breakfast was simple: buttered white bread with Rogers' syrup, cheese and grey coffee — which was three-quarters coffee, the rest cream. On Thursdays we had pancakes and on Sundays we had zwieback, cracklings and honey. Each of us had our respective places on the wooden backless benches on both sides of the varnished plywood table. We boys sat at one end and the girls at the other, according to age.

After breakfast we sang songs in High German, which none of us could understand till we were six or seven and going to big German school. But that didn't matter. The important thing was that we learned to sing them together. It was the same with the prayers. A silent prayer around here is not good enough. It has to be spoken so that the neighbours can join in. If we pray together, we'll stay together, Kleinsasser Abe-vetter the preacher often reminds us in his sermons.

The little school-ankelen, especially my Rachel-pasel, insisted that every child contribute with the singing. She always walked round and round the table, urging us along. And what a voice she had! I'm sure people could hear her sing from a quarter mile away at the garages on the north end of the colony.

After half an hour of singing and praying, we played. Toys were practically nonexistent in little school. It's different these days, because kids have more toys. Abe-vetter the preacher, he often warns the parents that they're losing their zeal on the narrow path. He especially disapproves of those plastic pedal-tractors which children ride along the cement walks.

---

* *ankela* (singular) *ankelen* (plural) is the Hutterite term for grandmother. It also is sometimes used for all older women (of grandmother age).

We had many make-believe toys. One of the boys' favourites was pretending to be airplanes: running about with the arms outstretched and making engine sounds. Another pastime was to loop a piece of baler twine around our thighs and gallop about, as if we were riding a horse. We'd slap or hinders with the twine ends and yell, "Gyddiyup, gyddiyup."

The girls, they had their dolls to play with: feeding, dressing, pampering and talking to them. I looked inside the hollow head of my sister Frieda's doll once when I twisted it off, and the huge eye sockets and the stubs of hair made me look away quickly. I thought I had seen the doll's brains.

At ten a.m. our little school-ankela carried our dinner from the community kitchen. We usually ate whatever the adults would have for dinner in the mess hall of the community at half-to-twelve. Mostly we ate perogies, *gashtel* soup, duck, chicken noodles, *maul taschen, shtumpus* and other traditional food that we still eat around here today.

"Eat so you'll grow big and strong," the little school-ankela urged us, making sure that we emptied our plates so as not to waste anything. For us boys growing up big and strong meant driving John Deere and Case tractors and GMC trucks. For the girls it meant cooking in the community kitchen, hoeing in the garden and helping their mothers with the chores at home.

At about eleven, we would all head for the sleep room where each of us had our respective pillow and sponge on wall-to-wall bunks that were a foot off the ground. The girls were on one end, the boys on the other. Our little school-ankela napped on a bunk nearby. After our nap, which lasted till one o'clock, we'd have a snack, sing and pray some more, play till three p.m., and then the day in little school was over.

Sometimes English people came to the colony. Kids

were not to go to an English car without their parents. If we did, and were found out or tattled on, our school-ankelen would have us reach out our palms the next morning and she'd lay a couple slaps there with her leather strap.

The only English words we knew were "Whatsye neme?" And there were words like penni, nikkel and kwutter. Whether they were German or English words we didn't know, nor did we question it. One thing was certain: English people who jingled money in their pockets were rich and they were likely to pass out a few coins. Unlike today, when some kids have piggy banks with a little chicken feed and even the odd loonie in them, it was rare to own even one penny when I was a kid. Whatever monetary allowance we got from the boss was carefully handled by our parents. Actually, later when I was already going to big school, my and the boys' average summer earnings of jaw breakers were worth more than our entire allowance for one year. The boss gave us one jaw breaker, the kind with a fennel seed inside, for every gopher tail we brought him.

Once, me, my brother Johann, Kleinsasser George and his sister Elizabeth sneaked to the root cellar, where a family of English people were waiting to buy vegetables. This was during the evening church hour, when our little school-ankelen's forever watchful eyes wouldn't be able to see us. Because we weren't six yet, we didn't have to go to church.

All those gum balls we hoped to buy from the Army and Navy Store on our first summer trip to Moose Jaw once we turned six and were going to big school crowded the fears of the strap from our minds. During the summer, boys — boys only though — were allowed to take one to three trips to Moose Jaw with their fathers. Girls had to wait for a doctor appointment.

At the English car, which was root beer-coloured, we reached out our palms to a half-naked English lady who handed each of us a coin that she fished from the bottom of her purse. I had to look away quickly when she swung open the car door and placed her sandalled feet on the ground. I had never before seen a grownup's bare legs and shoulders, and I was embarrassed. I also felt sorry that she might have to go to hell because she was being so sinful: walking around in broad daylight with hardly any clothes on.

Kleinsasser George, who was always the greediest kid, was angry because he had the smallest coin, so he suggested that me and him trade. Like a fool, I gave him my nickel and took his dime. But he wanted it back the next morning. Fortunately, my mother already had it locked away in a jar inside her chest of drawers.

In the fall, at potato digging time, which was also the beginning of goose butchering season, we made potato shooters from goose wing feathers. A potato shooter consisted of a hollowed out feather as thick and as long as a pen, and a tiny wooden syringe whittled out with our mothers' potato peeling knives. To load the shooter, we'd push each end of the tube through a half-inch slice of potato, then push one pellet through the tube with the syringe, which caused the pellet on the other end to shoot out with an audible pop. A good potato shooter could shoot a pellet clear across the living room. But after a couple days of wiping pellets off the walls, my mother usually banned our potato shooters from inside the house.

In the fall when I was five, all the kids in the other families — for reasons I've forgotten — had potato shooters before me and my brothers and sisters. But we weren't about to be left behind! After little school me and my brother Johann and my sister Frieda ran away from our baby-sitter and sprinted across the colony yard to the goose barns. We hoped that our fat Michael Wipf-vetter, who was the gooseman at the time, would give us feathers. We detoured past the shoe shop on our way because we were scared of Andy Kleinsasser the shoemaker. He liked scaring kids when they came to pick up shoes that he had repaired. Bogey monsters like "Grey Anna" and "Bingle Yewd" were always lurking around corners or in attics ready to spring on naughty children. My mother gave him heck when we came home crying a couple times.

"You leave my children alone!" she scolded him, waving her finger at him. "You hold your business with your shoes. Disciplining my children is their parents' and their little school-ankelen's job, not yours." And she complained to old Samuel Hofer, who was still the first preacher of Old Lakeville colony back then. But never-the-less, we were always cautious about getting close to the shoe shop.

As we neared the goose barns we saw that the gate stood wide open, yet Michael-vetter was nowhere in sight. So we walked right in. In our anticipation for potato shooters, we had forgotten that live geese would be large and grown-up, and not mere furry goslings that went "pip pip pip" when we held them, and that sometimes deposited a moist little present in our palms or on our clothes if we squeezed them too hard.

Mostly, I remembered large flocks of ugly-looking yellow-grey goslings grazing in the meadow near the garden dugout or in the bar pits. In the spring, Michael-vetter had given each of us one jaw breaker for every five-gallon pailful of grass we plucked from the banks of the sewer creek near the granaries, to feed his littlest goslings with.

But at the age of five I hadn't yet learned much about wild and ornery ganders! We were scarcely in the gate, when a grey and white wave of geese came sweeping toward us, half walking, half flying. Their outstretched necks seemed to come straight for our throats as the three of us shrank into a corner. They ruffled their feathers and wagged their heads about, shouting back and forth amongst themselves in goose language. Some of them hissed like my aunt Rachel's steaming clothes iron. I thought for sure we'd be gobbled up like the bad wolf had devoured the piglets in "The Three Little Pigs" story. But fortunately, my Michael-vetter came running to the rescue when he heard the commotion, and the geese fled.

When I was eleven, my vetter promoted me

from the garden. One of his previous helpers, Joseph Waldner, had turned fifteen and was promoted to the field. For the most part, me and my vetter's other helper, Amos Kleinsasser, were dedicated to our job. We faithfully kept the wooden troughs full of barley chop, the floats in the water troughs clean and functional and drained and pressure-washed the cement duck pond once a week. And in the spring, we herded the goslings in the meadows and in the ditches. It was a privilege to be stockboys, we thought. Unlike the gardenboys, we didn't have Andrew Hofer-vetter, who was the German school teacher and gardenman till I was twelve, watching every move we made during the summer. Which of course gave us more opportunities to get into mischief.

The chickenboys and the cowboys got extra bold one summer when they improved their slingshots by converting them to guns. Like usual, me and Amos Kleinsasser weren't far behind.

The way we made this slingshot gun was: we nailed the slingshot handle to the end of a thirty-inch piece of one by two. To the other end we nailed a double stock, made out of half-inch plywood. And we twisted a quarter-inch hard surface welding rod to form a cock and trigger, then bolted it into the stock. A spring, which we took off the Massey Ferguson combine parked at the scrap pile behind the feedlot, held the trigger tight. To load the gun, we'd pull the leather sling back and over the cock of the trigger apparatus, then place a smooth stone or bearing ball inside.

Deadly accurate this type of slingshot gun was! And powerful! Mostly, we shot tin cans off fenceposts, but one day when my Michael-vetter had gone to Regina, we cornered a gander. Amos Kleinsasser, he aimed to hit the gander in the chest, but his hand was unsteady because he was so excited and he hit the gander in the head. With a single squawk, the gander stiffened up and sank to the ground like a sack of potatoes. We thought that he was dead for sure, and for a minute there we stood frozen in our tracks as if 110 volts had passed through us. This was one of five breeder stock ganders my vetter had brought all the way from a *Shmiedeleut* Hutterite colony by Portage La Prairie in Manitoba. Of which he was very proud. My heart felt a lot lighter when the gander stood up after a minute and waddled off, although swaying like a drunk person. I prayed and hoped that he wouldn't die. That day we put our gun back in its hiding place underneath the straw bales and didn't touch it for three days.

Frank Hofer, who was a gardenboy till he got out of big school because his father was the gardenman, he was a spy, and he tattled about our guns to his father and that was the end of that affair for a while. The harder than usual strapping we got was was a reminder for a long time to think twice before making another gun. Amos Kleinsasser, he didn't feel much pain though. He timed it right and wore four pairs of underpants and six sweat shirts underneath his black clothes on the day of the strapping. But strangely, I felt good inside even while rubbing my burning seat, and better yet after Andrew-vetter had burned our gun in the ash barrel in the schoolyard. I'm afraid of guns. Every time I fired the slingshot gun, I felt part of something dangerous and violent.

When I was still in kindergarten, my Michael-vetter's geese were frequently harassed by coyotes. They'd run back and forth outside the fence, howling like demons. When geese get spooked, they pile up in a corner and many end up suffocating. When my vetter lost seventy-five geese in two nights, he got fed up and got permission to borrow a .22 rifle from Earl P. Kirk. our English neighbour. And he waited in the dark for the coyotes for three nights in a row till two in the morning. But no coyotes came. It might not be true — some people say it's just another of my vetter's tall stories; he has a habit of stretching up stories — but two nights after he had given up and taken the rifle back to Earl, the coyotes struck again. Only this time they got right into the pen.

Miraculously though, they never harmed a single goose. In the three nights that my vetter had been standing guard, he had propped a plank against the spruce board fence to lean on. But he had forgotten to remove the plank. So three coyotes had walked up the plank, jumped into the pen and were circling the inside of the fence, trying to get out. The geese were all bunched together in the centre of the pen. By the time my vetter got hold of the .22 rifle again and had it loaded, the coyotes had leaped over the fence and were gone. To this day my vetter claims that this really happened.

One time me and my sister Frieda and Kleinsasser George and his sister Elizabeth had a close call with a whole pack of coyotes. Or at least that's what we thought. It must have been in late September or early October because it was after potato digging time and the boys were already wearing winter caps and the girls were wearing their neck-kerchiefs. We had chased a stray cat all the way to the far side of the big schoolyard, which was surrounded by a barbed-wire fence and a row of caragana hedges. That's where the chase ended, because the cat darted towards the horse creek, which lies a few hundred feet behind the schoolyard. The creek got its name many many years ago when Old Lakeville colony had about forty horses. They were let loose back there before the land was broken up. In the summertime we had often gone down to the creek to pick saskatoons, pincherries and chokecherries with the older kids. But ever since my older brother Tim and the boys had seen coyotes running about in broad daylight back there, the south edge of the big schoolyard had been our border. According to my brother, the coyotes had their dens in the rock piles on the field.

I don't remember whose idea it was to howl like coyotes when the big school kids came out to play baseball at recess. Quite likely it was George's idea, because he was always thinking up ways to bug kids like Frank Hofer and his cousins Hofer Becky and Hofer Peter in little school. But anyway, we crept through the spaces of the barbed-wire fence and stood just behind the caragana hedges, grinning devilishly, intent on scaring the wits out of the big school kids.

"Yip yip yooo oooo ooo, yip yip yooo ooo ooo," we howled. And we waited and listened; my heart was clappering all the way to my throat.

"It's coyotes!" someone shouted. "They're right behind the caragana trees!"

We howled again, only louder that time. There's the old story about the shepherd boy who yelled wolf a few times because he was lonely, but in the end nobody believed him any more, so when the wolf came for real, he was eaten alive. Well, in our case, things never got to that stage. I took one glance at Kleinsasser George and the girls and I knew something was wrong after we had let loose our second succession of howls. We all looked at each other wide-eyed as if we had just seen and heard the devil. I dared look behind me. Suddenly the creek, the fence and the distance between us and the stubble hills weren't enough. I was certain I saw three or more coyotes amongst the grey-white rocks on the field, rushing towards us. And I was certain I saw the coyotes' fangs gnashing together and their red tongues licking the air, as if wetting their pitchfork sharp teeth with which to rip us to shreds. The others must have gotten the same picture because when I started running, they were right behind me.

Fortunately there was an opening in the caragana hedges nearby. All four of us burst upon the ball diamond, not daring to glance back as we scrambled for safety. With three or more assumed coyotes just inches behind us, howling like crazy and ready to take a bite out of our hinders, we raced past the big school and we didn't stop till we were out the gate. In our panic we hadn't even heard the big school kids laugh themselves foolish. And I'm sure if we'd have listened, we'd have heard their laughter echo off the school house and off the caragana hedges and off the horse creek out behind.

There were many things we had to be careful of when I was a kid. Frogs were one of them. If a kid touched one, he was sure to get a hundred warts. In the spring, as soon as the snow was gone, a kid with warts on the fingers would bury a piece of thread or string with as many knots tied into it as he had warts. When the string rotted in the ground, the warts were supposed to fall off. One time my mother got tired of me chewing on the wart on my thumb, so she clipped it off with her button hole scissors and bandaged it up with gauze and handy tape. Boy, did I howl!

Another thing we were never supposed to do was let a frog see our teeth. We believed that frogs counted peoples' teeth and as many as they counted would fall out shortly. And never was a person take a pee on the middle of a road, especially the one leading to the chicken barns. The danger was that he might get a chicken eye (sty). The only remedy, if a person did happen to absentmindedly pee on a road, was to spit out quickly. That was supposed to stop the chicken eye from starting.

In the spring when we were four, me and Kleinsasser George were inspecting a large mud puddle in the summer fallow behind the chicken barns one day. Halfway through, we started sinking and before we could waddle out, our rubber boots were sunk so deep in the mud, only an inch was showing above the water. So we bawled for half an hour there, till my baby-sitter found us and pulled us out.

Two Saturdays later this same place created more action on Old Lakeville than many of us had ever seen. First, the 1010 John Deere tractor got stuck with the honey wagon when my father, who was the chickenman then, was cleaning out the manure pits underneath the cages in the laying barn. My Paul Paul-vetter ran off to get a bigger tractor, the 706 International, which they hooked to the 1010 with a lugging chain. In my mind I can still see the diesel smoke billowing out black as the night from the mufflers of both tractors as they jerked back and forth there, cutting deep ruts in the mud. But the 1010 wouldn't budge from its grave. Finally my father realized that the 706 was stuck as well. By then about twenty kids and grownups had come together to see what the commotion was about. The next tractor that was brought to the scene was the 1175 Case with dual tires on it. The men hooked the tractors together, and all three tractors lurched forward, flinging mud cakes fifty feet into the air. There was so much noise with all three tractors revved up high, my father was afraid that the chickens inside the barns would get spooked.

"Bring the diesel!" Father shouted impatiently when the fellow in the 1175 also threw up his arms, and jumped out of the cab. "This is ridiculous!" Only once before had I heard a swear word slip from my father's mouth, but that day he muttered a few, like "*Gaaspuuck*!" "Devil!" and "For-sonava-gun-sakes!!" I felt sorry for my father, and ashamed because he had said these words.

The diesel was an old caterpillar tractor with a huge blade in the front with which the men bulldozed rock piles into holes or pushed deep snow onto piles in the winter. We could hear its metal tracks clanging along from where it was parked near the tractor garage and it wasn't long till it rumbled to the scene. By then, practically the whole colony, even a few grandmothers, had gathered to see the show. Some of the kids wished that the diesel would get stuck too so that the excitement could go on all day. I wished that this was the cowman's problem rather than my father's, so that I could wish the same.

But the diesel got praised to high heavens that day! It groaned and puffed only slightly as its tracks gripped the dirt underneath it and pulled the 1175 out of the four-foot deep ruts it was sitting in. After this, the men lengthened the chain to get onto dryer ground and together the 1175 and the diesel hauled the smaller tractors out as if they were as light as feathers. I remember arguing with Kleinsasser George about who would drive the diesel when we grew up. But by the time we got of age to drive big tractors, the diesel had long been replaced by the Case payloader, which has rubber tires.

But still, when the endless chattering sound of the geese drift through the late summer nights, and when the howls of coyotes echo from creeks to rock piles and back, the goose bumps on my back come forth. And I remember those geese, those coyotes, those English people, those tractors, those slingshots, those potato shooters and all that stuff.

STORIES ABOUT MY
MICHAEL WIPF-UNCLE

There are people — though not many — like my
Michael Wipf-vetter from Prairieland colony by Swift
Current, who seem to take life less seriously.
According to what I've heard about my vetter, he
was a real *tauga nixer* when he was younger. And I
didn't arrive at that conclusion merely from what
others have said. My vetter admits it himself. In fact,
he seems quite proud of having been a mischief-
maker and a ne'er-do-well. Most people his age
wouldn't admit to having been out of line with the
colony when they were younger. I figure that's
mainly because they don't want us younger people
to be able to rub it under their noses. In my
estimation, most of my uncles and aunts have turned
stricter with age. Some of them are always ready to
deliver a lecture, because the sermon says it's their
duty. When my brother Tim, who's left Old Lakeville
colony and lives out in the world now, comes to
visit, he's guaranteed five-minute lectures from at
least six people, including my parents and
Kleinsasser Abe-vetter the preacher.

   "So what's wrong with a little fun?" Michael-
vetter says to people who he thinks are too serious.
And he doesn't seem to care if his statements offend
someone or not. "Cripes, you gotta lighten up a little
these days. We're not in the sixteenth century no

more."

People have complained about my vetter and said he's been a raw egg since he was a kid and probably always will be. They say if he was a good Christian he wouldn't be making the crazy statements he makes; if he was to get elected to the preacher position, then maybe he would turn himself around. Daniel Hofer-vetter, the first preacher of Prairieland colony, who was my vetter's comrade when they were growing up, has warned him that he ought to keep his laughter and his joking under control; he's not a kid any more.

But to lecturers like that he replies that maybe he's weak, but cripes, he's trying his darnest; it says in the Bible that some were given ten pounds, others were given only one, and it ain't none of his fault God gave him only one pound. And he's not talking about pounds as in "fifty pounds of flour". My vetter is a big man and a heavy man at that, well over 250 pounds. And he jokes about his weight, which really bothers other people with weight problems.

"When I step on one of them scales," he says, "the kind that gives you your fortune, it shoots me out a note telling me that it can't function when two people are standing on it. Well, usually I try again, and it shoots me out another note, this one saying, no trucks please." And he tilts his head back and laughs like crazy and leans his entire body against the back of his chair, making it creak as if it was about to snap like a toothpick. He's known in several colonies as Fat Mike, the one who wrecks the chairs.

The best way I can describe my vetter is that he's got a personality like that fat actor John Candy I saw once when me and the boys hot-wired the field truck and went to Moose Jaw to watch a movie called "Uncle Buck" at the Capitol Theatre. My vetter has his beard shaved real thin and narrow, except at the tip of his chin, where it curls under like an upside-down duck tail. His nose is shaped like a small light bulb, and his eyes, which are dark like sandy soil, seem to be laughing all the time. On his

74

cheek, not covered by his beard, he has a long scar that he earned in his late teens trying to play a trick on *his* vetter, who was the field boss of Old Lakeville colony at the time. Michael-vetter sneaked up behind the half-ton, carrying a jack, intent on jacking up the rear end of the truck while his uncle was napping in the front between shifts of loading the hay wagon.

"I would've been able to jack up that truck all right, but Sam-vetter, he woke up sooner than I expected," my Michael-vetter says when asked about his scar. "He started up the truck before I had a chance to pump the wheels off the ground and the jack went flying. That's when the handle hit me in the jaw, banged a hole right through my cheek and knocked a couple of teeth loose.

"I didn't play another trick on nobody for a while after that," he says, as he hooks his thumbs behind his suspenders and stretches them out as far as the elastic will allow, then lets them snap back. (I think he does that just to bug people.) His black pants he has pulled high up around his protruding stomach, making his suspenders look as if they were stretched around an inflated inner tube.

"Wouldn't want to crawl under no trucks today," he snorts as he pats his bouncing stomach. "Might get stuck under there — better stick to my carpenter job."

People who can't stand my vetter's audacity say that he's just putting on a show because he likes the attention; that's why he says things that are totally ridiculous.

"Too much foolishness that man has for his age," Hofer David-vetter our German school teacher says, who's as pious as they come. "Has absolutely no afterthought about what he says. Good riddance that he was put on Prairieland colony's side when Old Lakeville branched out last time. I sure couldn't stand to have him around; no amount of praying would keep a person out of the mental ward if he'd be living here."

My Wipf-ankela used to tell me and my brothers and sisters stories about Michael-vetter. I got the impression that she always stood up for her sons regardless of the mischief they got into.

"Your Michael-vetter," she'd say, her big eyes behind her thick glasses twinkling with amusement. "He has ways of getting on people's nerves. I was worried about him when he was a young man. That he never ran off out to the world surprised me and your * ol-vetter because he sure liked to read western books and worldly magazines. Me and Ol-vetter were suspicious that he had a radio hidden away somewhere, although we never found it. But in spite of all the mischief he's done and no matter what people have said about him, your uncle is a kind man; never says an unkind word behind another person's back. Laughs a little too much, he does, but he's really a good person."

One incident that Ankela had a hard time forgetting was when Michael-vetter was arrested by the RCMP. About twenty-five years old then, he had taken a load of hogs to Moose Jaw with one of the International trucks that Old Lakeville used to have. These trucks had a habit of backfiring when the ignition got turned off while the truck was revved up high. Michael-vetter thought it was funny to drive down Main Street in low gear and let off a series of window-shattering explosions and watch people freeze up with shock and clutch their chests as if about to fall over and have a heart attack.

"I was so worried about my Michael when he didn't come home that night," my ankela said. "And when the police phoned out and said that my Michael was in jail I almost had a nervous breakdown."

A little while ago my Michael-vetter and his wife Rebekah came up to Old Lakeville colony to visit. Already when he drove into Old Lakeville he was full of folly. He stopped the Dodge pick-up truck he was driving when he saw me pulling into the yard from the west side with the 4040 John Deere, pulling the manure spreader. He rolled down

---

* _ol-vetter_ is the Hutterite term for grandfather.

his window and pointed to one of the rear tires on the 4040. He had a real serious expression on his face as if he was warning me about a life-threatening situation.

"Wipf Elias, your tire is going round," he called out. "You'd better get it checked."

I caught on to his joke right away that time and while laughing waved my hand to brush away his wisecrack remark. But I sure was happy my vetter had come to visit again.

As far back as I can remember, when my vetter came to visit, he has stayed in our unit for the night. So in the evening at about half-to-nine, when it came time for a little lunch and some coffee my mother had prepared, my father fetched Michael-vetter from the other side of the colony where he was visiting in our cowman Samuel Waldner's house for a while.

When guests come to visit, everybody waits for his turn to ask the guest into his house for a glass of chokecherry or rhubarb wine, beer or pop, and to spend time visiting and telling stories. My father asks home the baptised men, my mother the baptised women and my unbaptised sisters the unbaptised girls; it's up to me and my brothers to ask home unbaptised male guests. The easiest way to find out about the latest crop yields, or what someone read in the newspaper about current politics out in the world or the latest gossip going around in the colonies is to listen for a while when guests come to visit. Especially guests like my Michael-vetter, who travels to other Hutterite colonies a lot, where he's well known for his stories. Depending on who you talk to, he's one of those who somehow end up being on almost every wheel that turns. But it sure is nice to sit down and listen to him talk and entertain us with all his stories.

There's one story he's told about a dozen times: about the time he bought some firecrackers. I have a feeling he's stretched the story to make it funnier; good story-tellers have a way of doing that. Me and my brothers and sisters begged him to tell us that one again.

"Now listen up, all of you," he began, clearing his throat.

I noticed that his eyes quickly swept across the room to make sure there were no preachers around before he continued.

"This really happened," he said. And he held up his hand, his palm facing away from him, as if he were making an oath, something that's not allowed in the colony. But he always does that when he tells a real good one.

"That's the truth, believe me, this really happened," he repeated, which made me question the accuracy of anything else he had said so far.

About thirty, maybe even forty pairs of eyes were glued to him and that many pairs of ears cocked to catch every word he said. Some of us, the oldest first, were at the table, which my mother and sisters had pushed to the middle of the room to make more sitting space; we had just sat down for some coffee and a little lunch. The others were crowded back, filling up the entire hall and living-room of our unit, waiting for their turn at the table.

My vetter slurped down a canned pear and some juice and crunched down a couple of soda crackers piled high with peanut butter. He patted his stomach and grinned like any *tauga nixer* would, reached across the table in the same breath, and gave the signal to my sister Frieda that he wanted his coffee cup refilled.

"Well, this happened when I was about sixteen years old," he finally began, stroking down on the tip of his beard. "Me and cousin Danny Hofer had just gotten out of school and we were glad to be out on the field already. Now, as I recall, when me and Danny were still German school boys we always made slingshots from fast rubber we cut off an inner tube. We were shooting blackbirds and gophers out in the cow pasture. But Paul Wipf our German school teacher, who everybody called Paulus Knaulus for a nickname, he caught us with them slingshots. A real strict teacher that Paulus Knaulus-vetter was! The penalty for possessing a slingshot

78

was a lot harsher than for merely not being able to recite our verses or being loud at the dinner table. No, for this he'd use a caragana strap on us. And he'd make us read aloud two chapters in the New Testament or two sharp songs about the fire of hell and the thunder and lightning of Judgement Day. But me and Danny — you know how it is with boys, everything goes in one ear and out the other so fast you can hear the words whistling past — we got ourselves in trouble so often with one thing or another, I betcha we spent one out of every five days cooped up after German school for punishment on the mischief we'd done. We'd have just enough time to hurry home at five minutes before half-to-six and comb our hair and get ready for daily evening church service.

"To make a long story short — I know you can't wait to hear the best part — when I got hold of them firecrackers, me and Danny Hofer were out of school already and there wasn't much control Knaulus-vetter had over us any more. Actually, what I did with them firecrackers wasn't exactly what I had in mind when I bought them. The way I got them in the first place, an Indian hippie come up to me on the street in Regina; me and brother Albert were up there picking up combine parts.

"'Twenty firecrackers for one dollar,' he says to me. 'That's cheap. You can't get this good a deal no other place.'

"Well, I don't know if I got a good price or not, but when he blew one up in front of me, I figured I just gotta have them. So I *spritzed* my last dollar and bought the whole bagful.

"When I got home that evening I decided I was gonna wait for real good opportunities to blow up a few here and there and have me the pleasure of watching Danny Hofer and some of the other guys jump a few feet up in the air.

"Now, I ain't saying what I did isn't a bad and sinful thing to do, but when I stepped out of the house that evening after the sun had gone under, the first person I saw was Paulus Knaulus strolling

79

down the boardwalk, headed for the outhouse, carrying his roll of toilet paper and singing a religious song to himself.

"Well, the devil he came to me while I was sitting there on our steps and fingering them firecrackers and a box of matches in my pocket. And he gave it into my head about all the times I'd been strapped with Knaulus-vetter's caragana strap. I sneaked across the lawn to the outhouse after he had gone inside and I waited for about three minutes, giving him time to settle himself on the hole. Now I tell you kids, what I did was crazy — I figure because it happened twenty-five years ago, it doesn't hurt to tell about it — as long as you don't do such a thing today, okay?

"Anyway, I tied about ten fuses of them firecrackers together and lit them real quick, holding my hand over the flame so that nobody would see the light behind the outhouse, should anybody be peeking out the window. I pushed them through a little crack in the back, then sprinted into the night as fast as my legs could carry me. By the time the first one went off I had hid myself behind the pumphouse near by. The entire wad of firecrackers went off within five seconds of one another, and from the outhouse came an explosion that sounded like five International trucks backfiring all at once, and a scream of terror sounding like a sow being led to slaughter filled the air and echoed from one house to another. Paulus Knaulus, he charged out of that outhouse like a mad bull, tearing the door right off its hinges. With short and jerky steps he lurched towards the house, screaming like a frightened monkey, at every few steps tripping over his pants, which were zigzagging back and forth on his ankles.

"'My God in heaven!' he screeched, 'Judgement Day is here! *Olela, ma lieber himbel*...I'm not ready yet. I'm sure to go to hell!

"Right away the strains of evening singing that had been drifting through the open windows of people's units became silent and the whole yard was suddenly lit up as curtains were whisked aside and people stared out into the dark, wondering what in the love of heaven the commotion was all about. I don't think Paulus Knaulus had ever pulled his pants on as fast as he did then. With lightning speed, he grabbed his suspenders and the top of his pants and yanked them on to hide his shame.

"You might wonder how everybody found out the truth about who had done this. Well, my Maria Waldner-aunt, who in her day never missed as much as a person walking across the yard, always peeking out through the cracks of window blinds and from behind corners, she exposed me even before I could stretch up a story. It didn't take long before your ol-vetter came after me swinging his strap."

My vetter gulped down the last of his coffee after swishing it back and forth in his mouth and he looked about the room. He had grin on his face, as if someone had just complimented him for doing a good job of building a superb piece of furniture in his woodworking shop. I think my vetter gets great pleasure from hearing people laughing about his stories, the louder the better. And everybody in the room was sure bouncing up and down, making so much noise, my mother quickly closed the window so our laughter wouldn't be carried across the yard to other people's houses. Even Hofer David the German school teacher, who had just walked into the room to visit a bit — out of obligation I figure — couldn't resist smiling a little.

The look on my vetter's face got me thinking about another of his stories he had told us of when he was about five years old. He and his friend Danny Hofer went for a walk to the garages one day, which took them past the cow barn. The cowman of Old Lakeville colony at the time had a blue heeler, who was considered dangerous. This dog had got loose and he jumped in front of the two children, barking ferociously.

"Me and Danny, we were so scared, we started shaking like Jello and bawling in terror when we saw Chief in front of us, barking and curling his lips," my uncle Michael-vetter had said. "I tried hiding behind Danny and Danny tried hiding behind me, so we kept going in circles there, howling as if we'd just been strapped. Chief, he got confused after a minute of this, confused maybe about who was supposed to scare who and he took off, his tail between his legs. When me and Danny saw that our bawling had scared away Chief, we couldn't believe our eyes and we started laughing, suddenly feeling brave and about ten feet high. After that, no matter what, I never was afraid of Chief no more. But this sure taught me an important lesson, which I made sure I wouldn't forget. There ain't hardly as good a way to overcome a problem as laughing and joking right in its ugly face. Let me tell you one thing kids! If you can laugh at your own worst problem, you got it licked."

I figure my Michael-vetter is living proof of what he says about laughing making pain go away, even though laughing *too* much is a sin against Heaven Father. I wish I could laugh at everything a bit more, like he does, even though he laughs a lot at other people's expense.

I noticed my vetter's wife Rebekah was getting uneasy after he was done telling the story about the firecrackers.

"That's enough, Michael," she said. "We could puke already from your stories. Let somebody else talk for a while. Okay?"

My Michael-uncle hooked his suspenders with his thumbs and let them snap back as he looked around the room.

"Okay. So who's next?" he asked. "Which one of you knows jokes?

HOLY MAN'S DAUGHTER

The reason I went along was because Kleinsasser Abe-vetter needed help with the driving. He gets cramped knees when holding his foot on the gas for too long; all his sons and their Kleinsasser cousins had gone to a colony out by Calgary for two weeks helping remodel houses for their aunts.

"You're afraid of my father, that's why you don't want to come along with us, isn't it?" my girlfriend had said the night before, poking her finger at my chest. Her firm nature she inherited from her father was sure obvious in the tone of her voice.

I opened my mouth to make another excuse why I didn't want to make the trip to Saskatoon, but she interrupted me.

"Every time his name comes up, I can feel you pull yourself inward and you become quiet. And you hardly ever speak with him. Elias, if you really cared about me — and my family — you'd come along. You whisper into my ear all the time how much you love me, so here's your chance to prove it." She was silent for a moment; I caught the glassy flash of her eyes in the semi-darkness of the little school house we were in as she turned from me and looked out the window at the yard light nearby.

"Liz, I hold nothing against him," I said in an apologetic voice. "Me and your father just don't have much to say to each other."

"Well, maybe it's time you started."

"Couldn't your Peter-vetter go along?" I asked. "That's a long trip, three days, and staying in a motel with your father, in the same room yet."

"He won't bite your head off, you know."

"He might do worse," I said, making a joke. "He might give me one of his lectures."

"Maybe you deserve one," Elizabeth said. And she boxed my arm with her fist, then gave me a hug.

I sure had lots of time to think about what my girlfriend had said as we drove north along the Number Eleven highway on our way to Saskatoon, with only a foot of space between me and her father on the front seat. We were travelling to visit Elizabeth's Maria-pasel from Rose Hill colony by Davidson, who was in the University Hospital with Parkinson's disease. The doctor had said she didn't have long to live. Elizabeth and her mother, who's also named Elizabeth, were in the back seat of the crewcab, talking back and forth amongst themselves and Kleinsasser Abe-vetter while cracking sunflower seeds.

Abe-vetter doesn't seem to believe in talking excessively. At least not about material things; he's much too *Christlich* for that. Words coming from his mouth that don't have spiritual undertones are few and far between.

I had to admit that Elizabeth was right. I was afraid of him. The sermon says a person shouldn't have man-fright, he should rather have God-fright. But Abe-vetter *is* our first preacher, and I figure a person needs to have respect for a man of God, even be a bit afraid. After all, he *is* the one who reads the sermons to us, and he *is* the one who Heaven Father chose to lead our colony.

And that's all fine by me, but what bothers me is this: what business do I have, like a real *towga nixer*, being in love with a holy man's daughter? Now that's perfectly all right too, but I'm in love with her sometimes in ways of which the sermon says is sinful and yields punishment. At first, when we started going together, I was satisfied with holding her body close to me, feeling the pressure of her moist lips on mine, resting my hand on her clothed bosom and stroking the pretty flowers there. But my thoughts, like birds, kept landing, making my hands undo buttons. In his sermons, Kleinsasser Abe-vetter says a person can't keep a bird from flying overhead, but he can sure keep it from building a nest in his hair. I doubt I'd have enough strength for that even if Elizabeth wasn't standing guard and chasing those birds away. But still, a few twigs have found their way into my hair, and Elizabeth's too, just never enough to build a whole nest. Come baptism time we'll have to confess that to Abe-vetter so that our sins can be washed away. Boy, I sure don't look forward to that day.

I discovered how big a nest the birds would be allowed to build when I ploughed my conscience under one time and walked real casually into Leonard Fysh drugstore in Moose Jaw to buy me a box of condoms, even though my heart behind my ribs was clappering along at ninety miles an hour. But Elizabeth, she slapped me when I hinted clear enough for her to figure out my intentions, and for a few days there she refused to go on dates, or walk with me to the dugout and back in the moonlight; I had to write a few love letters to warm her heart.

Elizabeth, she doesn't hide her feelings. She candidly says her opinion right in a person's face without blinking. Exactly like her father does, who of course channels his frankness towards delivering a lecture, whether it's expected or not. And Elizabeth sure told me where I could go — I'm not proud of what she called me — what I had in mind was too much *verboten*, condoms or no condoms.

"Elias, you'll just have to wait," she said, wearing her father's stern *blick*. "If my father found out we were doing *that* before we're married, he'd for sure be in the grave within a week."

But no matter how firm my girlfriend is, she can sure be romantic, and I know she's the one with who I want to marry. There's nothing like quiet time spent with my Elizabeth in the little school, where we go after the sun has gone under and people have pulled shut the curtains in their windows. After bouncing on the tractor all day long, a man needs a woman to get his head back into forward gear.

Elizabeth is a couple inches taller then me, exactly five-foot-six-inches. Her hair is black like top soil after a rain; her cheeks are round and full. A bit fat I guess, but that's okay. Her body is like her face, and she has wide hips. My sisters say I'm biased when I say Elizabeth is the prettiest girl in our colony.

I first had a crush on her when I was only fifteen, in my last year of English school, and she was only fourteen. One time at recess, I was on third base — never could catch a ball mind you — and Elizabeth was determined to run home to win the ball game for her team. Like usual, I was trying to catch the ball as if it was the moon, that's how her brother Kleinsasser George described it. Elizabeth came charging at me with all her might, her legs pumping her then very pudgy body forward with a force as if propelled by a four-wheel-drive tractor or something. She landed on top of me, flattening me to the ground, and her lips touched mine — we both had bruised lips after that. But that was the first time I'd ever had a girl lie on top of me, and strangely, it felt good, even though it felt like my ribs were all broken. From then on my heart accelerated every time she came near me.

And it was beating fast now, as I was driving the crewcab to Saskatoon. But with Kleinsasser Abe-vetter that close in the picture, and thinking about the three days we were to spend together, I wasn't sure if it was love, fear or guilt that I was feeling. The brief thank you he had given me for helping him out like this made me feel somewhat better, but my feelings towards my future father-in-law were still far from ideal. In the year and a half that Elizabeth had been my girlfriend, only once, very briefly, had Abe-vetter acknowledged to me about going together with his daughter. As if it was something that needn't be talked about. I had asked Elizabeth what her father thought about me and her going together.

"He doesn't say much about these things," she said. "But I know he cares. I've seen him read the sweetheart cards you give me, and he smiles quietly to himself. And he says, 'if that's who you want, that's good, just be careful what you do when you're alone together.'"

I wondered what he was thinking about now, sitting next to me, straight and proud like a grain elevator you can see for miles and miles on a prairie. He seemed so *Christlich*, with his black beard and his black hat, his coal-like eyes looking up and down the wheat fields passing by.

"Now, that's a nice wheat field out there," he said from time to time, pointing to a field that was just turning to a slight gold under the early August sun, while he continued cracking sunflower seeds.

"Yup, it sure is," I said.

"That gives for sure a thirty-forty bushel crop, Heaven Father willing."

"At least," I replied.

"Here, take some," Abe-vetter said as he handed me the syrup pail of roasted sunflower seeds.

A few miles past Davidson my girlfriend, who, like I said, likes being romantic, puckered up her thick, firm lips and blew me a silent kiss — noticing I hadn't said much during the whole trip — when her father had his eyes closed and was napping a little. Through the rear-view mirror I saw old Kleinsasser Elizabeth smile knowingly to herself, and a warm feeling filled my heart and my whole body as if I had taken a swallow of whisky. I felt like taking one arm off the steering wheel, reaching back, pulling my girl close to me and giving her a kiss. But I didn't dare. Once in a while Kleinsasser Abe-vetter's eyes would flutter open when another vehicle whooshed past us and I was almost sure that if he caught me and his daughter kissing right under his nose, in broad daylight yet, he might not be very pleased. Like the time we went picking chokecherries near the Moose Jaw Air Base, to make wine with. Usually on such outings, all twenty-five or so of us unbaptised and unmarried young men and women pack into the colony's green school bus and Kleinsasser Abe-vetter comes along to keep us in line.

As soon as we were parked, most of the girls disappeared into the bush with the guys to pick chokecherries as far away from Abe-vetter as possible and to drink a little brewed whisky they had brought along, maybe even do a little romancing out there in the bush. But Elizabeth, she's not the kind of girl to do things in a sneaky way.

"There are plenty chokecherries right here," she said when I jerked my head in the direction away from her father. "Why go running all over the place?" She stood her firm body next to a bush hanging thick with the fruit and started plucking, and the chokecherries went plick plick plick on the bottom of the ice-cream pail tied to her waist with a long cloth belt.

I gave in; Elizabeth has control over me I can't resist. Besides, it's not often a guy is able to work side by side with his girlfriend other than in the slaughter house when we're butchering chickens, geese or pigs, or the other odd occasion. And even then you can't really say or do much because of all the eyes and ears close by. It doesn't look good to show too much emotion and affection and stand out in front of a whole colony of people and have people say: "That Wipf Elias, he's such a *towga nixer*. Around him you have to be careful."

Maybe it was the crisp country air out there in the bush, or maybe it was the spritz of Chanel perfume on her bosom that caused romantic feelings to stir inside my heart as I was standing next to Elizabeth and plucking chokecherries. I slipped my arm around her waist and pulled her close to me when her father went to dump his first pailful of chokecherries into the wooden boxes in the bus parked at the road. But you know how it is when kissing the sweet lips of your sweetheart, it's not so easy to pull yourself away and time seems to stand still. I didn't even hear the rustle of bushes behind me, I didn't hear the coughing at first either.

"Ahemmm, Ahemmm!"

I whirled around like a top, dropped my almost full pail of chokecherries to the ground and saw the preacher standing only five feet away. His dark eyes seemed to be boring into me like a drill, and my blood suddenly felt frozen.

"Keep yourself under control," he said. "This is not the place, nor the time for that."

He didn't have to say much more, his scowl said it all. He has a scowl — I've never said it in front of Elizabeth — that can stop anybody in his shoes from fifty feet away.

"He's only doing what he believes is his duty," Elizabeth said when I complained about her father always being on my and the boys' case, giving us his stern *blick*, as if he didn't trust us further than he can throw a hundred pound sack of potatoes.

"Why does he have to make a big deal out of us kissing out here?" I said through my teeth. "The way he looks at me makes me feel like such a ne'er-do-well. Can't he for once have a smile on his face and show at least *some* approval?"

"You're just imagining all these things about my father," she said. "He's not as stern as you make him out to be in your mind."

"Well, why is it that practically the only words he ever speaks to me and the boys are lectures? A guy gets tired of that. Maybe it's his fault I feels so spiritually inadequate in front of him all the time. I've never once heard him laugh!"

"So you'd rather have him be like your Michael-vetter, is that it? How much respect do you think you'd have for my father then?" Elizabeth said in a firm voice.

I had to admit, she was right about that. Abe-vetter is unlike my Michael Wipf-vetter as a clean forty bushel wheat crop is to an uncultivated summer fallow allowed to get infested with kochia weed, wild oats and quack grass all summer long. People have said that every second word my vetter says is horse manure and purposely said to cause laughter; that he has little respect for the colony. If suddenly he was voted to preacher, it would take many a sermon reading to change the image people have in their minds about my vetter, and start taking him seriously.

I was still thinking about the differences between my vetter and Kleinsasser Abe-vetter later, in the evening, when the preacher was signing his name on a piece of paper in the office of the Budget Motel in Saskatoon. He was standing at the desk, straight and poised, his Hutterite black hat and jacket a sharp contrast against the white wall of the office and the colour TV playing a comedy show with people "laughing sinfully," as he called it later when he unplugged the TV in our room.

"We'll get a room with large beds," he had said at home, when my father, who's the steward of Old Lakeville colony, counted out cash to pay for our trip. "There's no need to get two rooms and waste money."

"How many people are there in your group?" the short lady at the desk asked Abe-vetter as she raised herself on her toes and looked past him and out the window at our crewcab.

"Four."

"How many rooms will you need, sir?"

"One will do," Kleinsasser Abe-vetter said. "How many beds do you have in a room?"

"I can give you a room with two queen-size beds in it. Would that be okay?"

Abe-vetter turned his face towards me, then back to the lady at the desk, then back to me again.

"You don't mind if me and you share a bed, Elias, do you?" he said. "My wife can sleep with Elizabeth in the other bed."

"I...I guess that's okay by me," I lied. The truth was that I wasn't very thrilled with the thought of sharing a bed with Abe-vetter, even frightened. I had shared a bed with my Wurz cousins plenty of times when visiting at Fairfield colony down in Montana. But this was different here. This was with a preacher, whose daughter I was going together with. My brother Johann has often said that I babble on and on about Elizabeth in my sleep, and I smack my lips as if I was kissing her.

"Sometimes you hug your pillow as if it was a girl," Johann says. "And you murmur love words to it."

I cringed at the thought of waking up in the middle of the night with my arms around Abe-vetter, hugging him and deliriously mumbling love words into his ear. I mean, I wanted to feel closer to the man, but not that close.

"We'll take the room," Kleinsasser Abe-vetter said as he pulled his wallet from his pocket.

I lay awake opposite the preacher long after he had shut off the lights. My mind kept me awake for at least an hour, going over the situation many many times...how I could make more of an effort to come to more comfortable terms with my future father-in-law. By then Elizabeth, or maybe it was her mother, was snoring in the big bed at the far end of the room. I remember thinking how I would tease my girlfriend the next day about her snoring. But mostly I prayed that I wouldn't do any talking in my sleep that night. And that I would stay on my side of the bed.

STREAMS

There's something about spring runoff that's larger than life and makes me yearn for the times when I was ten years old. Back then, in the seventies, Old Lakeville colony had more snowfall in the winter than we get these days, or so it seemed. We had drifts so high we could step from the snow banks onto the roof of the chicken barn. And in March and April, when the drifts were melting, as usual me and the boys were outside with our snow shovels, digging out rivulets for the runoff.

It was easy to get excited about spring. The shifting and warming of the winds had blown away the icy sting of January, the insides of our almost forgotten snow caves had shrunk to ice, and cryptic icicles hanging from the ceilings were quietly going drip drip drip as if they were in some underground cave in a Hardy Boys mystery story. Cause for double excitement was when someone claimed to have seen the first crow on the naked elm tree in the cow pasture or a gopher peeking out of the hole in which it had taken refuge the fall before.

In our minds, spring had arrived when the snow drifts that the vicious and cold winter winds had packed hard against the barbed-wire fence in the bar pits had been softened by the chinook winds from the southwest and we no longer were able to walk on them without breaking through. Underneath, against the dead grasses, a stream would be forming, to emerge in a few days, at first gleefully bubbling forth where the snow wasn't deep, then melting itself a path as if it had a mind of its own, destined to go somewhere. The dugout maybe? The sloughs on the fields? Old Wives' Lake?

During this season it was always harder to keep the attention on the arithmetic and social studies in English school or the verses we memorized every evening for recital in morning German school. My mother didn't complain. I think she gladly accepted wet boots and socks, right along with the increased peace and quiet our absence from the house allowed her to have.

Of course the constant competition between us boys about any concern added considerable motivation to stream building. We were always competing over various feats: who could go the fastest with his sled, which group could build the biggest snow brick house or dig the longest and deepest snow cave in the winter, who was the first to catch a gopher and who could catch the most, who could fly a kite the highest, who could shoot the most blackbirds with a slingshot, or who could trap the most rabbits in the winter...the list went on and on.

The sides we took when digging streams were quite evenly divided: boys living on the west side of the colony against boys on the east side. The competition lay in which side could manipulate and bring together the most little rivulets to form the biggest stream.

Me and my brother Johann, our second cousins Kleinsasser George and his brother Steve, Barry Waldner and his brother Jason Waldner and a couple other boys were competing on our side. In this particular spring when I was ten, even our sisters pitched in.

"Elias, me and the Kleinsasser girls want to shovel out a stream too," my sister Frieda said as she and the girls came up behind me, each dragging a shovel.

I wasn't sure that letting the girls help was okay. I told Kleinsasser George, who had taken it upon himself to be our crew leader. He tried taking the shovel from his sister Elizabeth.

"Girls can't shovel fast enough," he said. "You'll only be in the way. Let us shovel alone. We don't need your help."

"Come girls," Elizabeth said. "He's just jealous. He's afraid we will make a bigger stream than they will. Let's make our own stream." And they trudged off and started scooping out a path behind the slaughter house alongside the outdoor vat used for cooking soap in the spring and scalding pigs when butchering.

"They'll get tired soon, then they'll stop," Kleinsasser George said.

Only a day later, much to our surprise, the four girls had dug out their own little stream. It angled towards ours and joined the main stream at the east end of the slaughter house. Me and Johann and the Waldner boys had been digging a foot wide ditch from a puddle about the width of the barn at the road leading to the chicken barns, hoping that once this was connected to the main stream we'd be able to gain the momentum needed to exceed our rivals' stream on the east side. The other boys in our group were busy routing a stream from alongside the cow barn and from the far end of the slaughter house. The plan was to bring all the streams together in the clearing in front of the cow barn and guide the water to the ditch alongside the road going north to the feed lot. Once there, it would connect with independent streams coming from the garages and the pig barns, all headed for the dugout beyond the cow pasture.

"You know, I think the girls' stream really helps," Kleinsasser George whispered. "Their stream is really running fast."

We were standing back, waiting for the signal for the evening church service and observing the progress we had made that afternoon. It was the kind of day when there were rivulets coming in all directions, man-made or otherwise. I'm sure if the water would have had the ability to think, it would have been saying to itself, "Gee, it's so nice of them to make a path for me, but I would've found my way out of this maze sooner or later."

Actually, there was no other way that the water could have flowed anywhere else but in the direction we were trying to guide it. You see, the plan the original people of Old Lakeville had was to landscape the yard in such a way so that no shovelling had to be done. Of course, nobody ever told us that, not that it would have done much good.

Now, when there is as much anticipation, work and competition involved in a job like we had, human nature provides us with a trait called cautiousness. And cautious we were! From day to day, we would send someone, usually Jason Waldner who was the youngest, to spy on the boys on the east side, and bring back a detailed report on their progress.

"Their stream is about the same size as ours," he reported back. "They've connected their streams up with tire tracks the chore tractor made."

After hearing this news, me and the boys held council and Kleinsasser George suggested that since we had very few tractor tracks in our favour, we ought to broaden our horizons and bring in streams from abroad. The first solution was to prospect beyond the chicken barns, which were the buildings furthest to the south. It was my brain wave to try coaxing a small lake that was fed by a ravine coming from the summer fallow hills south of Old Lakeville colony to send some water our way. We weren't quite sure whether Andrew Hofer-vetter, who was still the German school teacher then, would approve of this but decided in desperation for more water to risk the inevitable strapping in German school the next morning and an end to all stream activities as well.

"Let's all shovel like crazy," Kleinsasser George barked out orders. "Girls, we need your help, get yourself shovels, there's work to be done."

But alas, the water in that lake was lazy. It had its mind made up to flow west, completely bypassing the chicken barns, the slaughter house, the cow barns and our ditches we had so carefully routed for its benefit.

I suppose we would've accepted our fate and been content with having made a stream equal in size to the boys' on the east side if that indeed had stayed the case. It was at first, but not for long. Not that I'm making excuses on the west side's behalf, but the east side really had an advantage over us. It was only our stubbornness and our pride that kept us from accepting our fate. No, it wasn't that they had more visible snow on their side — we had more! We had several barns on our side that had helped trap high snowdrifts for us throughout the winter. All they had was a barn and the garden — and there wasn't much water escaping from the garden. The fate of that water had been decided long ago by the adults. Any water that was not usable was directed into the garden dugout at the south end of the colony, only a few hundred feet east of the big school.

But the other cycle, the cycle that had nothing to do with man's attempt to control his environment and nothing to do with man's limited ability to confine nature, had been in effect all winter, long before we started digging trenches. It had everything to do with nature's ability, like spirit, to give or take where it chooses to. That winter, we had had lots of snow.

The other boys' hope lay in the dugout. Not only did it collect runoff from the garden, it collected water from miles and miles into the hills. Thus when one cycle is finished, a greater cycle takes over.

Discouraged by the last attempt to make our stream bigger, our crew trooped off to inspect the dugout. We saw to our jealousness that the banks were already swollen and were groaning at the vast amount of water that was fast rushing into the dugout's hungry mouth at the south end. By now the water had almost reached the rocks at the north end. We could hear it lapping gleefully at the large rocks, as if planning its escape from this prison it had been guided into.

We prayed and hoped that the dugout wouldn't break.

"It's gonna run over this year." Kleinsasser

George's cousin Frederick said. He and his crew of shovellers had followed us to the dugout.

"I doubt that," Kleinsasser George said. "There's not much water left in the hills. The snow is almost gone."

We all looked out towards the south hills and then down at the churning water in the dugout. The hills by now had turned black, but in the lower areas there was still lots of white showing.

Frank Hofer from the east side started laughing. "My father says, when this dugout runs over it's gonna make a flood," he said. "And nothing in the world will be able to stop it."

Again we looked at the dark water, which was semi-calm as if brewing and scheming how it would escape the banks that held it.

The dugout broke the next day. It had been another warm day, and the south winds had licked the snow from most of the surrounding areas right to the ground. There came a roar and a whoosh from the dugout, as if the first wave was peeking over the edge of the rocks, shouting: "Here we come, watch out below."

The water swirled from the dugout in a wide stream, cutting a path for itself, taking with it any snow that was not yet melted. It rushed by, only a hundred feet from the longhouses, flushing away the thin and seemingly insignificant streams Frederick Kleinsasser and his crew had been making during the last week. At the road, it sat in the ditch at first, its body swelling by the minute, as if impatiently waiting for the culvert to let it pass, then with a final gush it rolled over the road and flowed towards freedom. We watched it hurry past the garages and into the ditches behind the garages and finally merge with our own well-nurtured stream at the feed lot. It swallowed our stream effortlessly and, as if energized by this added contribution, it cut itself an even wider path.

All throughout this episode of watching the water make a mad dash for the main dugout, getting stronger by the minute, the boys on the east side were waving their shovels in delight, laughing and laughing, running across "their river" as they called it, filling their boots and for a minute stepping out of the water to wring their socks dry, then once again wading into the water, testing its strength.

"We won, we won," they shouted over to us, who were standing by. "Our side beat yours. Your stream wouldn't fill up the dugout in hundred years. But ours...ours will fill it up in no time flat."

"To heck with this," I said, after reviewing the situation in my mind for a bit. "This is no more their stream than it is ours. I threw down my shovel, rolled up my pant legs and waded into the stream. The water's strength caught me by surprise and the icy liquid flowed over the top of my rubber boots. It stung, but it felt good. My comrades from the west side followed me. And all of us, east side and west side together, laughed and splashed around in the "river". It wasn't often that we had the opportunity to splash around in a wild river in southern Saskatchewan.

In the midst of all the excitement, Kleinsasser George drew me aside and said quietly: "Let's get our gopher traps out tomorrow and get a head start.

THE NICKLUS

Last Christmas Eve I was the Nicklus.

In previous years, I had taken on a "whatever will be" attitude about the whole affair, knowing that one of the other guys like Kleinsasser George or Jakob Hofer, who don't mind standing out in a crowd as much, would volunteer. For the last two Christmas Eves in a row the Nicklus had lost out because the young men and women of Old Lakeville colony had preferred spending the evening in the community kitchen, exchanging gifts and singing Christmas carols instead.

Strangely, the carolling and the gift exchanging hadn't seemed quite enough for me, and even after a couple shots of Peppermint Schnapps or Canadian Club whisky and cola, for which all the boys had pitched in to buy, I'd still go home feeling like I had missed out on something after the evening was over.

Sure, my mother — like she has forever — still filled up shoe boxes or ice cream pails with Christmas sweets for me and my brothers and sisters. And still, like I did when I was a kid, I ate my entire assortment of goodies in the three days of Christmas and in the days between Christmas and New Year's. I gave my girl Kleinsasser Elizabeth a set of Corningware dishes and a pair of shoes, and received a couple of shirts and some socks from her. And me and my brothers gave my mother and father and sisters each ten or twenty dollars to spend at Woolco or Army and Navy in Moose Jaw.

But it's not the same without the Nicklus tradition. At my age of twenty-three, and in the days of getting older and supposedly wiser and nearing baptism age, a guy sometimes wishes he could've stayed a kid a bit longer.

"I think this year we should have a Nicklus," I had said to the boys, a week before. "Without one, it doesn't seem like Christmas no more."

All the families of Old Lakeville were gathered in the mess hall of the community kitchen that morning to receive our share from the truckload of Christmas stuff that my father had brought from Regina the day before. Me and Kleinsasser George, Jakob Hofer, Barry Waldner and a few other guys were standing around flirting with the girls while waiting to carry home each of our family's portions.

"Are you gonna be the guy who gets dressed up?" Barry Waldner challenged me. We had just joined the lineup at the mountain of peanuts, where Kleinsasser Abe-vetter our first preacher was shovelling family portions into plastic pails.

I wasn't prepared to give a definite "yes", but just in case the idea blew over like it had the last two Christmas Eves, I allowed as much. "Who knows, I might be interested," I said. "But if someone else wants to do it, that's fine by me too."

"Wipf Elias, I think you're the man for the job," my second cousin Kleinsasser George said, with a smirk on his face.

"How do you mean?" I asked.

"With your looks Eli, you could scare even the devil," Barry Waldner cut in. "We wouldn't even need to paint your face or nothing, all you'll need is the sheepskin coat and you're in business."

"I dunno about that," I said, raising my chin. "I've heard that some of the girls think I'm the best-looking guy of Old Lakeville colony." I put my arm around Kleinsasser Elizabeth's shoulder while her father wasn't looking. "Isn't that right, Liz?" I asked.

Before Elizabeth had a chance to answer, Barry and the boys and a few of the girls who heard that let out a laugh so loud that everybody in the hall turned their heads and Kleinsasser Abe-vetter shot a frown in our direction.

"Now, now, keep your laughter under control," he said. "We're not world people here, okay."

I think it was the Red Rose tea at supper time on Christmas Eve that really got all of us thinking about Christmases when we were kids and got us all hyped up once more about having a Nicklus. At Old Lakeville, we have tea for supper only a couple times a year on occasions like Christmas Eve and the Eve of Good Friday, using fancy china that's used only for celebrations.

"Wipf Elias promised he's gonna do it this year," Kleinsasser George announced. "It's his turn anyway."

Actually, in my mind, I had already agreed to do it a few days before. After supper, me and the boys joined the girls while they were finishing the dishes in the community kitchen and the married women had gone home. Katrina Hofer dragged out an old sheepskin coat, the kind that men from Old Lakeville used to wear in the wintertime many years ago. My girl Kleinsasser Elizabeth dug up a pair of knee-high felt boots and an old floor mop that I was to wear on my head, and my sister Frieda brought over some make-up and lipstick she had hidden away somewhere.

I was surprised that the sheepskin coat still had the original wild smell of wool and tannin on it that I remembered from when I was a kid. Back then, long before Christmas Eve arrived the threat of the Nicklus would be in the back of my and my brothers' and sisters' minds along with the mounting excitement of the season as we learned our Christmas verses.

In German:

Papa, Mama, nun ist der tag
Der liebe, gute Weihnachts mann
Drum sag ich auch ein wünschlein an

101

Ich mächte gern auf erden
Ein gutes kindlein werden
Will stets die eltern lieben
Und niemal sie betrüben
Will artig, fleisig sein, und fromm
Damit ich in dem himmel komm
Amen.

Papa, Mama, now is that day
Of that loving, noble Christmas man
Hence I do announce my wishes
So I might gladly, on this earth
Become a child of virtue
Will constantly love my parents
And never cause them grief
Will strive for good behaviour,
Diligence, and piousness
So that into heaven I will come
Amen.

We'd recite these verses before receiving our shoe box filled with chocolate bars, candies, chocolate-coated marshmallow Santa Clauses, nuts, cookies and bubble gum with comics inside, all of which my mother so generously lavished upon us on Christmas morning. Sometimes, if we were lucky, my father would give a new toy truck or some Lego blocks to me and my brothers, and dolls to my sisters. And all of us together would receive a new five-thousand piece jigsaw puzzle which we assembled during the Christmas holidays.

When in English school, all the children picked a gift from the Eaton's or Sears Catalogue and on the last day of school, as part of our Christmas program, our English school teacher Mrs. Graham brought us our chosen presents. They'd be nicely gift-wrapped and stacked under the Christmas tree, the only Christmas tree in the entire community. At home, in the houses, there weren't any decorations besides maybe a string of Christmas cards that we received from relatives and friends from other colonies.

Christmas at Old Lakeville is celebrated over three, sometimes four, Sundays in a row. On each day there's a two-hour church service in the morning and Sunday school in the afternoon for all unbaptised members six years of age and older, and an hour prayer service in the evening. And in the homes, every family continues the celebration by singing *Weihnacht Lieder* and reading from the Bible about the birth of Jesus.

Anyway, it was my turn to go to Moose Jaw to deliver eggs to our customers on the last Thursday before Christmas. I was curious about where the Nicklus tradition came from, so I headed for the public library later, rather than join John Wipf our chickenman for a Christmas shot of whisky with Ralph and the boys at Southern Automotive, who are some of our regular egg customers.

In a large hardcover book with many glossy colour pictures about Christmas in it, I read that Nicklus got started with St. Nicholas in somewhere called Asia Minor. Many years later the St. Nicholas tradition was brought from the Old Country and eventually became Santa Claus. Somewhere down there in the mid-atlantic States, groups of Dutch and German descent shared two Christmas figures - the *Christkindl*, an angelic child messenger of the new-born Jesus, who often carried the gift of a tree, and *Pelznickol*, a scary Nicholas dressed in furs who carried switches to frighten naughty youngsters. He also carried a bag of toys and treats. But the book didn't say anything about how *Pelznickol* got started in our colonies. I assumed that because our forbears lived in Russia for some time before they came to North America, they too adopted some of the traditions of the Dutch-Germans who came from Russia, and chose *Pelznickol* to discipline children, calling him Nicklus.

On the Christmas when I was five years old, there were two Nickluses. All day long in kindergarten school me and the other children stole troubled glances out the window and often checked each other's pulses to see who's heart was pounding the fastest in anticipation. Our little school-ankela sure didn't relieve our anxiety.

"Sshhhhhhhhh," she said, pointing to a trapdoor in the ceiling that led to the rafters. "Listen, it's the Nicklus...he will carry naughty children up into the roof." We listened carefully, our eyes wide and our bodies pressed against the wall, as if it could offer protection.

And at home, after supper and after it got dark, we avoided getting too close to the windows. The Nicklus had been known to lurk around corners outside. When there came a knock on the window, we shrank back and huddled against the bed nearby, ready to take refuge underneath. We had heard that the Nicklus was too fat to crawl under the bed after us. My mother whisked aside the curtain and we saw, pressed against the glass, a wild face showing large, wide-open and bulging eyes and menacing teeth and a shrivelled nose. Me and my brothers and sister let out screams of terror and in a flash were on our bellies underneath one of the beds. Of course, this was only Hofer Sam, one of the big school boys who went around to a few houses with his sister Clara, knocking on windows and making scary faces by stretching out the corners of his lips with his thumbs, pulling his cheeks down with his index fingers and pressing his nose against the window.

"Get going on home," my mother warned him, wielding a yardstick at him as she yanked down on the cord to roll down the blind. "We don't need you sliming up our windows."

The real Nicklus came later, with the adult boys and girls, and they didn't knock on any windows. My older brother Tim, who felt brave enough already to look out the window, gave the signal when the Nicklus wasn't far off.

"They just left the kitchen," he reported. "They're going to the Kleinsasser kids' house first."

It wasn't long before the muffled thud thud of the Nicklus jumping back and forth, the wailing of children and loud laughter came through the walls. All of us: me, Tim, Ida, Frieda and Johann, were trembling, huddled together against the back of our living-room bench, anxiously gripping the bottom, waiting for the knock on the door that meant it was our turn.

"I'm not going to be afraid," Tim said, nodding his head assertively, trying to be brave. "I'm not going to cry, I'll show that Nicklus."

But as the screaming coming from the Kleinsassers' unit got louder, he made a dash for the bedroom, hoping to make a last attempt to crawl underneath the bed. The door was locked.

"You'll all see the Nicklus," my mother said. "It will do you much good."

My brother Albert, who was then only a year old, was sitting on my father's knee, oblivious of anything out of the ordinary.

"He's not smart enough yet to be scared," my father said. "If he does get upset, I'll hold my hand over his eyes."

My father placed a yardstick at his side just in case the Nickluses got too rough with us, but still, everybody who was old enough not to have bad dreams at night because of this would have to see the Nicklus.

Then suddenly, after a short lull, the girl carrying the bell in front of the crowd was in front of our door. The loud clang clang of the bell and the sharp knock on the door broke the nerve-wracking silence and sent a wave of panic through my body, accelerating the pounding of my heart all the way to my throat. The door opened slowly and the girl with the bell pushed her head inside. Grinning wickedly, she swung the door wide open and rang the bell again. Then the boys and girls spilled into our house, bringing with them the cold from outside, their perfume smells and their chewing gum smells. Any moment now, the Nicklus would jump into our midst! And he did. The crowd spread a little and in one cat-like leap the Nicklus landed in the middle of the room.

"WWWWHHHAAAAAAAAAAA!" he roared like an evil creature. He then started running back and forth between me and my brothers and sisters, glaring wildly into our faces.

105

"Are you going to behave from now on?" he shouted as loud as the giant in Jack and the Beanstalk. His face and hands were black with chimney soot and his eyes had red circles drawn crudely around them. His lips were also smeared with red, and on his head he wore a grey mop, the long cord-strands dangling in his face and down his neck. He wore an English man's pants, the legs pushed into his knee-high felt boots. And he wore a long sheepskin coat. The leather, which was on the outside, smelled wild, like a sheep.

"Yes, yes, yes, yes, yes, yes!" I managed to stutter between cries of terror as his hideous image swam into my vision. "I'll behave! I'll behave!"

"And do you promise not to fight with your brothers and sisters?" the Nicklus roared, his large hands clawing the air in front of me.

"Yes, yes, I'll be good, I'll be good, I won't do anything bad!"

"Not so rough, Jake," My father warned as he raised his yardstick.

Then suddenly without warning the second Nicklus jumped from the crowd. This one had on a black sheepskin with the wool turned outside. He wore a Hallowe'en mask on his face and a witch's hat on his head.

"GGRRRRRRRR, GGRRRRRRRRRRR!!" he roared, glaring at us through the slits in the mask, which made his dark eyes seem like the devil's. That's when Tim bolted forward, crawled underneath the table and wrapped his arms around the leg closest to the wall and Frieda buried her face in my mother's lap. But the Nickluses dragged them both forward. The second Nicklus lifted Tim, who was bellowing loudly, onto his shoulder and carried him up the stairs going to the trapdoor to the dark attic. In the back, the crowd was cheering them on.

"I will behave! Let me go! I'll be good from now on!" Tim cried out.

"Okay, that's enough," my father said, after what seemed like fifteen minutes, although it was probably five. "Get going now." He swung the yardstick in the air and lightly hit one of the

Nickluses on his hinder.

Slowly, the Nickluses and the crowd filed out the door, and everything was suddenly very quiet except for me and my brothers' and sisters' sobbing.

"Okay, it's over now," my father said. "And the Nicklus won't be back till next Christmas." But he added: "Unless you don't behave or cause trouble for your mother."

Ten minutes later, the fear of the Nicklus had faded somewhat, and it was almost gone — though we kept away from the windows — after my father pulled a few boxes from underneath the washstand and said: "Look what the Nicklus brought for you!"

"How do I look? Do I look scary enough?"

My girlfriend Elizabeth and my sister Frieda were smearing black and blue make-up on my face and dark red lipstick on my lips and around my eyes.

Someone held a mirror in front of my face. When I saw my reflection, I laughed. The mop sat on my head like a lump of spaghetti and my face had wild streaks of make-up paint on it which looked like the first watercolour painting I did in English school when I was seven. I felt silly, dressed like that, as if I had been caught walking outside of the house in broad daylight wearing only my pyjamas. Yet I felt like a kid once again, excited about Christmas, but also afraid. Even though I was on the other side this time. The Nicklus himself.

SHOES

When I was still a kindergarten kid, me and my brother Johann and my sister Frieda used to go down to the chicken barns in the afternoon after little school, and we thought that we owned the chicken barns more than the other kids at Old Lakeville colony because my father was the chickenman. And we assumed we knew more about the English people who came to buy eggs than the other kids did. We sometimes got the opportunity to get real close to them when my father invited them into our house for a glass of rhubarb or chokecherry wine.

"This is good wine," they would say, their eyes glassy as they held their wine at eye level as if toasting something. I assume that's what they said, I can't be too sure. None of us were able to understand any English other than "whatsye neme?" until we were seven and going to English school. My sister Ida had taught me how to read and write from Dick and Jane books she had brought home for me. That was pretty much the extent of my ability to understand English.

Anybody who drove a car (an English car of course, because Hutterites don't drive cars; only vans, trucks and crewcabs) and spoke English was considered an English person. All of us who were living in the colony were *Deitcha leit* (German people) and the rest of the world were the *Englisha leit* (English people), except for one egg customer who spoke Bible German, as my mother explained. At the time I couldn't yet understand this language either because until the age of six, when I started going to German school, all the German we spoke was our everyday unwritten Tyrolese German.

About Indian and Chinese people, we weren't sure. All we knew was that they looked different, yet most were dressed in English clothes and spoke a language that was presumably English. Later, in English school, I somehow got the picture (through books) that Indians lived in teepees and hunted buffaloes on their painted horses and scalped English people. From sources other than books, mainly from observation and listening, I got the impression that Indians got free peanut butter and sardines from all the other English people, were no good and all they did was drink whisky all day long. And I thought that Mexicans were extremely lazy and you could never trust them, Eskimos all lived in igloos and were very ugly, Ukrainians were dumb and Chinese all owned chop suey restaurants, made soup out of chicken feet and ate little else but rice and half-fried vegetables. As for all the types of English people in general, because they were not living with us in the colony (we who at the end of the world would all go to heaven), they would simply have to go to hell. I never was quite sure where exactly Mr. Hildebrandt, the superintendent of our school district, would go at the end of the world. He spoke Bible German as well as our Tyrolese German. The only problem I could see was that he wasn't living in a colony.

Sometimes a bus load of kids from the city came to tour our colony. Some of them knew so little about the farm we could actually convince them that the calves in the cow barn came from large eggs, the chickens grew on trees and the planks and two-by-fours in the carpentry shop were grown from plank plants in our garden.

But shucks, when a person is just a kid, so what if there are a few things he doesn't understand.

But I sure wondered about certain things a little while ago when a famous politics man from the city toured our colony. He ran a fistful of wheat through his hand and said: "Gee, this is nice looking flax."

But what really, I mean really, made me wonder, was what happened one time when I was in a store in the city. I had walked into a store (a big store it was) to buy my girl Kleinsasser Elizabeth a birthday present. This was on just a typical Thursday, when many of us from Old Lakeville colony, Caronport colony and even from a couple colonies by Swift Current come to town to deliver eggs, bring in a load of hogs or potatoes, or visit the doctor.

There weren't many people in the store at the time. I was standing behind a shelf in the shoe department, near the cashier counter. My girlfriend, she had been complaining the shoes she was wearing weren't very comfortable, so I figured if I bought her another pair, her problems might go away.

I doubt that the lady behind the counter knew I was there. You see, I hadn't exactly walked in there and announced my presence by shouting: "Hark hark, Wipf Elias has just arrived in town and he's about to buy his girl a pair of shoes."

So I was just standing there, trying to remember if it was size six or size seven shoes that Kleinsasser Elizabeth wears, and regretting not having it written down on a piece of paper. I mean, how dumb can a guy get? Walking into a store to buy some shoes for his girl who he's going together with for two years since he was twenty-one and not even sure what size shoes she needs!

Anyway, just then a group of Hutterite women and children breezed into the store. Right away the cashier lady, she started speaking on her loudspeaker.

"Mr. Merchant, could you come to the cashier, please."

It took less than a minute for a man to come huffing up to the counter. He wore a suit and tie; a real sovereign looking fellow he was. Had his hair all spritzed up real fancy and clean looking. It didn't take me long to figure out he must be the store manager or something close to it. I could see them through the shelf, but they couldn't see me.

"It's Hutterites. They just walked in. A whole bunch of them," the cashier lady said, pointing in the directions of where the group of women and children had dispersed. Some had headed for the Homeware section, others for the Electronic department and some to the bargain bin in the middle of the store.

"Yvonne, you stay here," the lordly looking manager half whispered and half barked. "Keep an eye on these ladies at the bargain bin; report to me if you see anything suspicious. Those in front of the TVs are okay; all they're going to do is watch soaps. Alert Melissa in the Homeware section."

He had barely finished giving orders when another group of Hutterites from Old Lakeville colony strolled into the store: five ladies, one man (Hofer David-vetter our German school teacher) and four or five children.

The manager twisted up his face, away from our people, and he started fidgeting like a rabbit that's just been cornered. He slapped his hand on the counter, grabbed the loudspeaker phone and softly spoke into it. But I could see his face clearly from behind my shoe shelf blind and I noticed his expression matched his voice like a pair of feet with a white shoe on one foot and a black shoe on the other.

"Phoebe. Aisle number ten in Homewares. Jeff, come to cashier number two."

He turned to our people who had just walked in, nodded his head in greetings, his hands he had in front of him, his fingers interlocked.

"Hello there, can I help you with anything?" he said through the grin he had planted on his face.

"Just looking sir," Hofer David-vetter said, stopping momentarily, then turning after the women who were headed towards the bargain bin.

I placed the shoes I had been inspecting back on the shelf and headed for the door. Halfways there, where the manager was standing, I looked up and shot a glare at him which I think he'll remember for a long time. I calmly walked out into the street, my eyes searching for another store that sells shoes. The fifty dollar bill in my wallet, which I hoped would cover the cost of the shoes, was wrinkled just a bit more when I found a suitable pair at another store. The shoes were brown, a shoe colour that's not allowed at Old Lakeville, so I bought some black shoe polish to fix them so they'd safely blend into the environment at home. I even had a little money left to buy myself a few Luke Short westerns at the book exchange store later. But I haven't been back to that store that has the manager with the spritzed up hair.

WATERBED

"But you just bought this waterbed from us four, five weeks ago, Mr. Wipf. Something wrong with it?"

That's what Ed O'Reilly the manager of Bart Quell Auction said when me and my Paul Paulvetter carried the waterbed through the door and set it down on the wooden floor of the second-hand store. He stroked his hand down over his horseshoe-shaped moustache and peered over the top of his thick round glasses, and he had a look on his face much like my father — who's the steward of Old Lakeville colony — has every time wheat prices sink lower.

"Ah, things have changed, Ed," Paul Paul said as he groaned and slowly straightened out his back. "We won't be able to use it no more."

I figure if anybody knows individual Hutterites' buying habits, it has to be Ed O'Reilly. He's been the manager at Bart Quell Auction for as long as I can remember. It's become habit, every time we go to town, to stop and browse through the store, even if we don't have any intention of buying anything. Which is most of the time, because we have very little pocket money to spend.

Ed, he brings in truckloads of furniture, TVs and radios, lawnmowers, shelves, fridges, almost everything a person could think of. Mostly what people from Old Lakeville colony are interested in is chairs and tables, frying pans, toasters, tools and toys, the kinds of possessions that aren't usually supplied by the colony and aren't officially allowed or forbidden. That's where things get sticky once in a while.

I remember the day when Paul Paul-vetter bought the waterbed.

"Brother Joe from Rose Hill colony says sleeping on a waterbed is like sleeping on the dugout," he said to me as he pondered over the frame and over the box which contained the rubber mattress. "I've been thinking of buying one of these for quite some time. Maybe it could help my back a little."

Paul Paul-vetter, he's had a weak back since just before he got married. About seven years ago he tried lifting an engine block from a little Ford chore tractor he was fixing off the ground and onto a metal sawhorse, and he strained some nerves in his back. That's why his back bothers him sometimes and he can't lift anything heavy.

My vetter isn't real short like me and Frank Hofer but his head doesn't stick out in a crowd either. His beard looks like a clump of grass on a lawn that's just been seeded, not because he styles his beard that way, but because the only place he can grow any amount of beard is on the tip of his chin. His walk is kind of funny: he lifts his toes off the ground towards his rear end with each step and he has his shoulders drooped and his arms hanging straight down, hardly swinging. His name is really Paul Wipf, but everybody has been calling him Paul Paul since he was a child. My * ol-vetter's name was Paul Wipf and two of his brothers had sons who were named Paul. So there were so many Paul Wipfs that they called my uncle Paul Paul, after my ol-vetter, to avoid getting them mixed up. That's the same reason people call me and my brothers and sisters by our last name first, like Wipf Elias and Wipf Albert, while my father's name stays the same: Albert Wipf.

---

*   *ol-vetter* is the Hutterite term for grandfather

Paul Paul-vetter got promoted to the job of shoemaker and also to the job of gooseman three years ago. There isn't enough work for a full-time shoemaker any more, because these days Old Lakeville colony buys about half of the shoes we need. Still, he can make one heck of a nice pair of western boots. I'd say his boots are as good as any others in the stores in Moose Jaw. Me and the boys pretty well all have a pair of western boots for dress that Paul Paul-vetter made. Of course, Kleinsasser Abe-vetter our preacher doesn't know that my vetter made them. The only boots and shoes that he's allowed to make are those that aren't too fancy and not too pointed at the toes. The thing about western boots is, like with a few other things, they're not really forbidden but they've never been officially allowed either. Abe-vetter sort of overlooks our western boots as long as we don't wear them to church.

"This waterbed here, it's eighty bucks, eh?" Paul Paul-vetter called over to Ed at the other end of the store. He was turning the price tag over and over, as if looking for something else written on it.

"What's it say on the tag?" Ed asked, looking up from his desk, where he was writing down something in an invoice book.

"Eighty dollars...is that the right price?"

"Well, if that's what it says, then that's the price. I'll tell you, that waterbed is in A-1 shape. At eighty bucks you're getting yourself one damn of a deal," Ed said.

Paul Paul-vetter was quiet for a moment, but he kept flipping the price tag back and forth between his fingers.

"You couldn't knock off twenty bucks, could you?" he asked.

Ed shot my vetter a questioning look and he raised his voice a little. "Man, at eighty dollars, you're already getting the lowest price possible. Jeez, Paul, I gotta make a living too, and you don't see me haggling over the price of your chickens and potatoes every time you boys come around selling them."

Paul Paul-vetter patted his wallet in his pocket. "All I got is sixty bucks, Ed," he said. "I'd pay you what you want for it, but that's all I got."

Ed got up and walked across the room. He towered above both me and my vetter and he had a weak smirk on his face.

"You know, Paul, between you and me and your friend here, you guys from the colony drive the hardest bargain of all my customers. You're shrewd buyers, you fellows."

"Well, when you don't have much pocket money, you have to be stingy with your cash," Paul Paul-vetter said. From the expression on his face I assumed he was joking around a little. My vetter is not really a joking kind of person. He's as serious as a preacher, as the saying goes. Not serious in ways of being religious like Hofer David the German school teacher, but serious about the principle of something.

"Listen, Paul," Ed said, "Maybe you can make me another pair of boots; a pair for my little girl this time, for her birthday that's coming up. You make me a pair and I'll give you this waterbed, no charge. What do you say?"

Paul Paul-vetter flashed me a nonchalant look and winked as if he'd been caught in some act and he was trying to be cool about it. He looked over his shoulders for a few seconds, and when he spoke he talked fast and in a low voice as if he was confiding in a secret matter.

"Sure, sure, I suppose I could do that. It would take me a couple of weeks though, 'cause I'm quite busy in the goose barn these days." It was obvious to me that my vetter would've preferred to make this deal with Ed privately.

It's no secret that me and the boys who aren't baptised yet moonlight for pocket money once in a while by trapping foxes and coyotes in the fall and winter or working out for our English neighbour, Earl P. Kirk. For that we get the regular penalty of standing up during the two-hour Sunday church service and getting reprimanded by Kleinsasser Abe-vetter or Andrew Hofer-vetter our preachers, in front of all the people in the colony.

"You've gone against the golden principle of community living so often, it doesn't register any more," my father warns me and my brothers Johann and Albert every time we get caught moonlighting for private gain. "You don't think now that it's serious, but you wait till you're twenty-six or so, after you're baptised. That's when the devil starts gnawing on a man's conscience and tempts him with the same addictions he had when he was young."

Once in a while, usually at Easter, a baptised person confesses to having earned money for private gain, just in time to be given the two-week probation and forgiveness before the *Abendmahl Lehr*, the Last Supper church service that only the baptised people attend.

I thought it best not to say anything about the deal that Paul Paul-vetter had made with Ed O'Reilly as we loaded the waterbed in the back of the crewcab and drove home. That's his business, I thought, and I'll just stay out of it. But I noticed that he was deep in thought and he blankly stared straight ahead at the road. I could see that something was bothering him. When he finally mentioned the waterbed and the boots, he seemed apologetic.

"Listen, Eli, I don't make these kind of deals often. I hope you don't get wrong ideas."

"Hey, Paul, what you do is none of my business. As you know, I'm not exactly innocent either when it comes to making money on the side."

"Sure, but with me it's different, you know what I mean." he said.

"Oh sure, I understand." I said.

Paul Paul-vetter seemed relieved to be talking about this, as if it offered some consolation to his troubled conscience. I knew how he felt; it helps to talk about something that's bothering you and it's always comforting to know you're not the only one doing something wrong. My father has warned me and my brothers and sisters about this sometimes. "Are you going to jump into the fire because everybody else has jumped in?" he asks.

"But you tell me, Eli," Paul Paul-vetter said in a sad voice. "Isn't a man kind of driven to dealing on the side when you consider our five dollar monthly allowance?"

"It sure doesn't reach very far, if that's what you mean," I answered.

Paul Paul-vetter sure didn't have much time to enjoy his waterbed. A couple of weeks later, when Kleinsasser Abe-vetter laid down his sermon book to close the Sunday church service, he leaned forward towards the benches and people and he gave everybody a piercing look before he continued preaching without the book in his hand. Everybody knows that when he does that, he's about to deliver a sharp lecture.

Twice a year both our preachers travel to a special meeting where all the *Lehreleut* Hutterite preachers come together to discuss various issues and trends, compare ideas and make sure that law and order is retained in all the colonies. At this meeting they set the standards for all the *Lehreleut* colonies and it's up to the individual preacher to administer them in his own colony.

So our preachers had just come back from a preachers' meeting at Cypressville colony by Medicine Hat.

"Beloved brothers and sisters of our community, we are living in dangerous times," Abe-vetter began. He was having a hard time keeping his voice from wavering and he pulled his handkerchief from his coat pocket and dabbed at his moist eyes.

"It appears that we are always walking on the edge. The devil, he will not rest and give us peace, and for the brothers and sisters who are weak and inclined to follow his ways, we must pray.

"Our dear elders have voiced their concerns and have pleaded for help in uprooting a serious and potentially dangerous situation that is fast taking over.

"It has been found that there are people among us who have succumbed to the carnal lusts that belong to the world and have brought waterbeds into their homes. These waterbeds, as our elders have pointed out, are primarily for the purpose of enticing sinful and carnal pleasures. It was our consensus that all waterbeds must be forbidden from hence forward and that anybody found with a waterbed in his home shall be subject to probation. Not only are these waterbeds sinful, but to obtain them means a brother or sister has to forfeit their baptism vows and go against the golden rule of community in order to obtain the money to purchase these beds. Isn't it enough that we have our regular beds which the community provides for us?"

Abe-vetter went on to cite other issues that were discussed at the preacher meeting, but the banning of waterbeds was the big issue people were talking about over the next few days.

So when me and Paul Paul-vetter carried the waterbed back into Bart Quell Auction, he didn't think it would do much good explaining to Ed O'Reilly why the waterbeds were suddenly forbidden. That's how it is. We don't bring these kinds of things out in the open and talk about them with people out in the world because you can't expect a world person to understand anyway. But Ed, he's a curious man and he managed to get quite a bit of information from us.

"What about your back?" Ed said. He seemed concerned. "Couldn't you complain and claim that the waterbed did your back a lot of good?"

"The truth is, it probably didn't help me anyway," Paul Paul-vetter said. "Besides, it's not worth the hassle and the attention. I'd sooner not stand out in the crowd and disgrace my family."

"So I guess I have to pay you back some money for the waterbed?" Ed asked.

"Well, maybe not," said Paul Paul-vetter. "Maybe I can find something I can trade for the waterbed."

"Sure, that'll be just dandy, Paul. Those boots you made for my little Jessica are superb, so you go

121

ahead, pick whatever you want and I'll decide on the limit." Ed made a sweeping gesture with his hand across the whole store.

Paul Paul-vetter's eyes roamed back and forth, searching amongst the furniture, tools and toys, while I fiddled around with a broken record player, not planning to buy it, but merely to pass the time. Ed picked up an electric frying pan.

"How about one of those?" he suggested.

"Naa, Magdalena has two of them already," said my vetter.

"Hey, I just thought of something," Ed spoke up excitedly as he headed to the far end of the store. "We got in a roll of carpet this morning that's in excellent shape; about five or six square yards."

Paul Paul-vetter's eyes flew wide open.

"Yeah, Magdalena can always use pieces of carpet to make floor mats for in front of the door and in the hallways."

I smiled quietly to myself. I knew, and my vetter knew also, that carpets covering the entire floor are officially forbidden at Old Lakeville because they're too worldly. But small mat-sized carpets in front of doors are okay. Or at least not forbidden.

TRIP TO MONTANA

Always, on those long trips to Fairfield colony down in Montana, my mother would pack an empty Rogers' syrup pail along. It had to have a lid, that's for sure. The kind that would close real tight, because when the smelly effect of motion sickness was deposited into it — which never failed — she'd thus prevent even the slightest discomfort to the rest of the passengers. That's how my mother is, always treading lightly, so as not to cause other people grief. And there never was a shortage of extra people who piled on board when the long awaited trip to visit our uncles and aunts came up.

I remember one trip when I was about seven years old. There was only room for two of us, one of the boys and one of the girls, besides my brother Sam, who was only a baby then and who'd be up front with my mother throughout the trip. Me and Tim and Johann pulled straws to determine who would go and Johann pulled the longest. But I sulked and moped around the house for four days, which caused my mother's nerves to become electric, as she described it, and her blood pressure made her head feel like a hot-water bottle about to burst. In the end she gave in and agreed to let me go along too.

"Oh, so you're starting a special trip to the States," Katrina Waldner from the old Isaac Waldner family said. "Well, since you'll be going past Medicine Hat anyway, after you drop off the Hofers at Plains Creek colony by Maple Creek, you might as well drop me and my Esther off at Cypressville colony, it's been so long since my daughter Rachel out there had visitors."

"Well sure," my mother said. "But just so you'll know, we for sure can't stop for coffee and to visit this time. We know how much your daughter will want us to step off for an hour or so — it already is thirty miles out of the way, both ways — all we have time for is unloading your baggage, then we have to keep driving. It's still a long way from Cypressville to Fairfield."

"Oh, we understand, we wouldn't want to hold you up," the Waldners assured her, like always.

This was my mother's and Hofer Barbara's trip; at least it was supposed to be. They were the only women from Old Lakeville who had married to Canada from colonies in Montana and they had waited a long time for the opportunity to get this trip rolling. My mother had been the one who asked Kleinsasser Abe-vetter the preacher for permission to go.

"It'll be so good to see my brothers and sisters again," I remember her saying often. "It's not fair, the number of times a year other people get to visit with their families and I have to wait so long because my sisters are so far away."

But in spite of my parents' plan we stepped off at Cypressville anyway. My father had to gas up there, otherwise we wouldn't have made it to our next stop.

"Only a *lopp* would let the vehicle run out of gas," he said. So while all of the passengers stepped off at Rachel Waldner's house — some of us needed to go to the toilet — he drove off to the gas tanks with one of the men. It took him longer than he expected because the steward of Cypressville colony had to walk all the way from the haystack out in the pasture, where the men were stacking hay, to give my father a receipt for the gas.

We hadn't been seated five minutes in Rachel Waldner's house when someone opened a bottle of orange pop.

"For the children," they said. "We know how much children love pop." And since it was baking day, Rachel Waldner sent one of the girls who had quickly gathered, to the community kitchen for some fresh-baked rhubarb pie.

"Bring an ice-cream pail full of *shneki* from the freezer as well," Rachel Waldner called after her. "I'll give you along some cookies and candies for the children," she said to my mother. "Mine always get so awful hungry while travelling."

At Cypressville colony we picked up more passengers. Two paslen and one boy already out of big school wanted to travel with us one way to Fairfield colony and visit an ol-vetter who was sick. And they'd be taking along a little baby girl, barely old enough to crawl.

"Sure," my father said. "Why not?"

Then of course, there was my Michael Wipf-vetter and his wife Rebekah and their kids who still lived at Old Lakeville at the time. Rebekah-pasel she married up to Old Lakeville from Coaldale colony by Lethbridge. To drop them off, we had to travel almost to Lethbridge, another thirty miles out of the way. Otherwise we could've travelled straight south from Taber along the Number Thirty Six highway towards the Coutts border.

The last ten miles to Coaldale colony were along a narrow dirt road that twisted and turned like a garter snake and climbed up and down some coulees like those roller-coasters me and my girlfriend Kleinsasser Elizabeth once saw on TV at the Co-op Store in Moose Jaw.

That road sure put me and the rest of the kids to the test. And some of us failed. It didn't take long for me and my sister Katie and one of Hofer Barbara's children to turn pale as we started firmly pressing our lips together and wriggling them as if chewing on something.

I started first, then Katie, and it wasn't long before Hofer Barbara's Thomas started, as if someone had turned on a faucet. Hofer Barbara too, pulled a can from her bag and passed it back to us. I don't know why they hadn't thought of giving us Gravol pills.

"No more candies after this," Hofer Barbara said, waving her finger at her children.

"Roll down the windows," my mother called out frantically to my father and my Michael Wipf-vetter as she handed my brother Sam to one of the ladies sitting on the seat behind her. To us she called out: "Hold your hand over your mouth and wait for the syrup pail!"

At Coaldale colony there was no question about whether or not we should step off and visit a little with Rebekah's family.

"You will stop here to wash the children's faces, have dinner and visit a little," Rebekah said, not giving us a choice in the matter. "You should fill up on solid, good food like *gashtel* soup and duck rather than candies," she pointed to us children. "That will make you feel better while travelling."

"Oh for darn sure you gotta step off and visit with my wife's folks," my Michael Wipf-vetter said. I think he had forgotten that because of him we had stayed twenty minutes longer at Cypressville than my father had planned to. Like usual, Michael-vetter started telling his humour stories to the people who had gathered. He's always been full of folly (some people call it BS or horse manure) and when he gets wound up telling his stories, a person has to almost tear him away.

"Holy smokes, we have hayhoppers in Saskatchewan this year!" he had said while slurping down coffee and wolfing down a wedge of rhubarb pie. "You know, the other day I was listening to the meadow larks up on my house's roof singing "spitz knittle hubigow," when I heard a roar like a million bumble bees. I looked up to the sky and the next thing I saw was a whole cloud of them hayhoppers coming from the west, right over Old Wives' Lake. Thank God our field man had them crops sprayed already, 'cause we'd have lost at least three wheat fields right there."

126

The people at Cypressville had shaken their heads; I think they knew already that you couldn't believe my vetter further than you could throw him.

Then there was the baggage. Apple cases and orange cases and pear boxes, tied shut with baler twine, full of God knows what (personal belongings, gifts and dry goods, they said at the border). To begin with, the van had already been loaded to the ceiling in the baggage compartment and we couldn't see out the rear windows when we pulled out of Old Lakeville in the morning. But that didn't keep people at Plains Creek and at Cypressville colony from depositing a total of seven more boxes — I counted them — into the van to deliver to people at the colonies we were to stop at. My father had to repack all the boxes in the back to make room for the new freight. What didn't fit, he placed underneath our feet, between the seats.

"Since you're going up to Fairfield colony anyway," an ankela at Coaldale said, hobbling up to the van with a cane. "My sister down there, she'll be expecting a box from me. Would you be so kind to deliver this to her?" And she handed my mother a box and a piece of paper on which she had scratched a few words about the contents.

"Sure," my mother said.

"There's some leatherette and a couple pairs of rubber boots we got real cheap in Calgary," said a young man, who came running with a box twice the size of an orange case. Me and Johann couldn't stop laughing at his black hat that looked like it had gone through an auger or mix mill a couple of times, and his beard was scraggly looking, as if someone had practised using a clipper on it. He came huffing to the van just as we were about to pull out of Coaldale colony. "We promised our folks down in Montana we'd send down the leatherette on the first trip. Since you'll be stopping there anyway to drop Hofer Barbara and her kids off, you might as well take them with you. You do have room, do you?"

"Well, I don't know," my father said, scratching his beard. He shouted back to where me, Johann and Katie and a couple of Hofer Barbara's children were wedged into the seat. "Is there room back there?"

There wasn't, but he managed to squeeze the box in anyway, in the space between the side door and the seat. If any of us children in the back seat wanted to get out, my father would have to open both side doors of the van and pull out the box first. Or we could climb over the seats after the two ladies and the two little twin boys in the seat in front of us had stepped out of the van. These passengers had come aboard at Coaldale colony, filling the vacant seat that my Michael Wipf-vetter and his family had occupied. Those two boys, they sure made a lot of noise, from the very start. They kept bouncing up and down with their feet on the seats, and making high-pitched shrieks of excitement.

"Lena and her children up there at Dunkirk colony will be so thrilled to see us," one of the ladies said to Mother as we pulled out of Coaldale. "We were planning to go down there at the preacher meeting next week, but this way we'll be able to visit longer."

"Oh, for sure, you are so wise to come with us," my mother said, looking straight ahead and smiling with her lips, but not with her eyes. She was rocking baby Sam from side to side. He had started to cry like a little lamb, and she had the type of look on her face that I knew only too well, because me and my brothers and sisters had provoked it often enough before. It was the look that said everything was okay, though it really wasn't. I found a high word in my Websters dictionary while I was thinking about writing down this story that I think pretty well describes how my mother felt: Claustrophobic. Sometimes my mother tries to explain her feeling. "It's as if my skin is wrapped in plastic and is trying to breathe," she says.

Long before we got to the Coutts border, my father was already drumming nervously on the steering wheel with his fingers and he was gnashing sunflower seeds faster than normal and spitting the shells into a syrup pail. He asked my mother to pour him some coffee from the thermos, to quieten down his nerves. My mother herself was shuffling paper slips back and forth, probably trying to arrange them in some kind of order, while holding on to Sam at the same time.

"Dear Heaven Father help us," she said, taking a deep breath, folding her hands in a short prayer and looking up to the ceiling of the van, as we rolled to a stop at United States Customs where the customs officer was waiting. "We got so much stuff to take over the *grenz*, I'm sure they'll throw us in jail."

"Just stay cool," my father said in a low voice, "I'll talk to the *grenz* man."

I remembered my father saying at home how much easier it is going through the border at Coutts than at the smaller borders like Willow Creek and Wild Horse further east because of the time limit. At Coutts, there'd be more vehicles needing to pass through in a hurry.

The officer peered into the van with eyes that seemed to be like knives, cutting into the boxes in the back and underneath our feet, exposing everything. They even seemed to cut into the plastic bag of candies that a nice lady at Coaldale had given to me and the other children. He looked intensely at my father, as if trying to see behind my father's sunglasses.

"Which part of Saskatchewan are you from?" the officer asked, his eyes still roaming the interior, stopping to focus now and then on the boxes wedged between the blue seats and along the sides with the light-green window curtains hanging limp on them. He was probably used to Hutterites travelling through, their vehicles loaded to the hilt with people and baggage.

"Moose Jaw," my father said, "and we have a couple of ladies and some kids from around Lethbridge."

The officer asked a few more questions and my mother passed the lists to him.

He read through them, shaking his head. "You planning to do some more shopping in the

United States?" he asked.

My father looked at my mother quickly, then back to the officer. "Oh, I suppose we'll do a little shopping," he said. From the look on his face, I could see he was relieved, as if a hundred pound bag of flour had been taken from his back, and he already knew that the officer wouldn't be going through our baggage.

After a couple more questions, the customs officer waved us through. As we entered the States and were far enough away for the customs officer not to hear us, one of the ladies we had picked up at Coaldale colony let out a sigh and she whispered something to her sister about "thank God the *grenz* man didn't check through our boxes." I made out a few words that sounded like "couple gallons of chokecherry wine and some brewed whisky." I figured that they had it stashed in the boxes underneath their feet between the seats.

We reached Dunkirk colony by Shelby in about an hour and a half, at near half-to-six, just as the people were preparing for daily evening church. There, Hofer Barbara and her children stepped off and my father unloaded their baggage. Her plan was to wait for her brother Andreas to drive up from Sunnyside colony by Havre that evening and pick them up.

The van suddenly seemed empty, like the way my mouth had felt once when I had lost three of my baby teeth in one week.

By the time we got all of Hofer Barbara's and other people's boxes unloaded, half an hour had passed.

"Remember, we cannot stop here," my mother had warned my father before we drove into Dunkirk colony. "If we stop here, we might as well stop for the night, that's how tired I am already. It seems like we've come a thousand miles today."

Hofer Barbara must have known how my mother felt. "Listen, Peter-vetter, they cannot step off here," she said in a real stern voice to a man who asked my father if we were thirsty and if we were ready to tilt down a cold beer after travelling so far all day. "These poor people — all we've done today is make stops all over the country — they have yet to travel more than a hundred miles, almost to Great Falls. Let them be on their way."

"Just asking,just asking," the vetter said, raising his palms.

We were sure tired by the time we got to Fairfield colony. All of us: me and my brothers and sisters, were stretched out or propped up and asleep on the now empty seats and when we finally drove into Fairfield colony. But when all our uncles and aunts and cousins — William-vetter, John-vetter, Maria-pasel, Susanna-pasel, Rachel-pasel, cousin Sam, the two Josephs, Paul, Phillip, John, Sarah, the three Marys, Peter and Leonard, Anna, Dorothy and many others — came running to the van, we were suddenly wide awake. This was the big moment we had waited for for a long time.

"Come, come inside for something to drink, you must be awful tired," John-vetter said. "We'll unload the van for you."

The trip, like always, was worthwhile, and the three days me and Johann and Katie spent playing with our cousins at Fairfield colony and getting spoiled rotten with all the goodies and attention our uncles and aunts gave us were like going to heaven for a little while.

But I remember, because I took note of it, how in the back of the van, a stack of boxes was accumulating. On the second day of our visit, the back was half-full already. Yet people from Fairfield kept bringing boxes over to my Rachel-Pasel's house, where we were staying.

"Since you'll be going to Coaldale colony anyway on your way back to Saskatchewan," I remember one tall pasel saying, who had come over carrying an orange case, tied shut with baler twine and with names written on the outside with a jiffy marker. "Me and my husband, we were thinking, if you have room, maybe you could deliver this box to my brother and his family up there."

"Do you have a list of what's in it?" my

father said. "It helps to have a list at the *grenz*."

"It's just some dishes and some cups we got real cheap at a sale in Great Falls."

My father coughed real loud to attract my mother's attention as the woman stood waiting at the door. But my mother seemed not to hear him. She was too deeply engaged in conversation with Susanna-pasel, something to do with a certain tricky dress pattern they were sewing together on Rachel-pasel's white sewing machine, and talking about the cucumber yield in the garden, all at the same time.

"*Och ma lieber himbel*, yes!" My father agreed. "We'll make room, just leave it here. I'll get someone to carry it to the van later.

BONESETTER

It's not the chrome-coloured oxygen tanks in the marigold bed outside his window, and it's not the rush trip to Moose Jaw with the Chevy van from which Mike Waldner our truck man had taken all the passenger seats to make room for the bed. It's not those nine hundred people who came to mourn till five in the morning, and it's not the black dresses the women were wearing on the day of the funeral. And it's not the dark hole either, that my Paul Paul-vetter had dug with the 580 Backhoe, into which we lowered the coffin. It's none of these things that bring back memories of my ol-vetter, even though they are the most recent.

What I remember best about my Wipf ol-vetter is how he fixed me up once when I had a dislocated shoulder.

I was twelve then. Me and Kleinsasser George and some of the other boys had made slingshots from fast rubber we had sliced from an old inner tube we had found on our neighbour Earl P. Kirk's scrap out on the field, across the creek from Old Lakeville colony, halfway to Old Wives' Lake. I was practising shooting little stones that I was picking off the gravel road behind the slaughter house and aiming them at my target. It was dark already, the best time for me to be practising and not get caught by Hofer David-vetter the German school teacher, who'd not only take our slingshots from us but also have us bend over in morning German school, where he'd warm up his leather strap on our taut hinders.

After a while I got tired of aiming at the smokestack on the scalding vat used for scalding pigs and cooking soap; tired of listening to the ping pong of the stones ricocheting off the metal stack and against the roof of the slaughter house. I felt like shooting something that moved. Well, along came Frederick Kleinsasser, who was a year older than me and almost a head taller, carrying water to his family's poplar trees.

Honestly, I intended to shoot only once, then scramble for safety in the dark. But the two or three stones I fired at him at first just whistled past his head by about ten feet. I wasn't a good enough shot yet to hit my targets from a distance. But I couldn't resist the temptation, so I sneaked closer, and he saw me. When I hit him, he let out a yelp like a puppy that had gotten its tail stuck in the crack of a door, flung his pails to the ground and charged after me like a mad gander.

At half-to-ten, my ol-vetter was in bed already. But my wailing that carried far through the still spring night caused my mother's nerves to become like electric, as she said later, and she sent my older brother Tim to call ol-vetter immediately.

"Tell him he's hurt real bad," she shouted after him. "He's crying like he'd been amputated on."

"Now how did this happen? And at such an hour yet?" Ol-vetter asked when he arrived. In his hurry he hadn't bothered to button up his shirt collar nor his black jacket, and I could see the untanned skin below his neckline. His blue eyes searched mine and his forehead was creased into question lines. Yet I detected a tone of amusement in his voice as he stroked his long and cone-shaped white beard. This I interpreted as a sign of confidence that he could heal me. After all, he was a bonesetter, and he had helped many many people before me.

"I..I...well..I...Fred Kleinsasser...he did it," I stammered, trying to avoid his eyes, which seemed to bore right through me. "He started fighting with me suddenly just for nothing behind the slaughter

134

house, and he yanked at my arm and twisted it back. I think he broke it."

"Ohhhhhhh, we'll have to show that Freddie Kleinsasser a thing or two, won't we?" my ol-vetter said in one long drawn-out breath. "Beating up my Eliasel for no reason at all." He usually called me and my brother and sisters by our childish names. "We'll have to tell the German school teacher about how that Freddie starts fighting with smaller boys for no reason at all and twists their arms so their ol-vetter has to rush from his cosy bed in the night."

His detached attitude didn't seem quite right and I didn't know what to think. I thought that he could have shown a bit more concern about whether or not my arm was broken, rather than question me about how it happened, at least for the moment.

"No, please...don't tell David-vetter," I said quickly. "Fred Kleinsasser, he said if I tell on him, he'll hit me so hard with his fist, it will knock me unconscious."

My ol-vetter sighed deeply again, but didn't say anything. He lifted my limp arm and gently swung it from side to side. At one point, he gave it a sharp turn and pushed it inward, and the joint went "gnup gnup". I felt a sharp pain burn into my bruised shoulder-blade, and I thought for sure my arm was broken in half. I started crying again.

"Okay, then maybe we should go over to Freddie's house right now and have him apologize for what he did to you," my ol-vetter continued, as if he had heard only half of what I had said. He began twisting and massaging my neck till it too went "gnup gnup gnup". "What do you think Eliasel? Do you think that would be the proper thing to do?"

I just held my frozen gaze at the floor, at the feet of my mother and my brothers and sisters, who were standing in front of me and Ol-vetter, watching him. He opened a jar, which he had pulled from his black satchel, dipped his forefinger into it and dug out a gob of smelly liniment, then spread it all over my right shoulder and neck. It stung like hot water and smelled like aftershave lotion mixed with some kind of grease in the truck garage.

"Elias!"

This time his voice was sharp and didn't have the hint of amusement in it. "Now look me in the eye."

He lifted my head up by the chin. "Why do you lie like this to your ol-vetter? Your poor ol-vetter, who was so generous to get out of bed — where you *towga nixer* should have been an hour ago already — to come and fix your shoulder.

"Why do you think you can fool me by lying up a story about Freddie Kleinsasser? Don't you know that lying is a terrible sin against Heaven Father?"

I was beat and I knew it. I guess you can't fool old people so easily; they know a few things we younger people haven't caught on to yet. I told everybody the truth. My ol-vetter patted me on the shoulder, the one that wasn't bruised.

"I'd bring my strap over right now and give you a few clips clops myself, for doing such an awful thing, Elias," he said in his stern voice. "But I think you learned your lesson. Now didn't you?"

I nodded.

I never really knew where I stood with my ol-vetter, nor did any of my brothers. He was the kind of person who'd be real stern like the strictest preacher around and give us a few clips clops on the hinder one minute or twist our ears into a knot, almost lifting us clear off the ground when he caught us doing something mischievous, then give us a candy or grab us by both shoulders the next and say something like: "Oh, my dear heaven, it's my Albert's Eliasel, and look how big he's grown already. He'll make a fine preacher when he grows up."

It was no secret that my ol-vetter had always wanted to be a preacher. He knew the Bible and our Chronicles in *Das Geshicht Buch der Hutterishen Brüder* as good and better than anybody in our colony. That's what my Wipf ankela said when she was still alive and we'd go up to her house to visit her in the evenings. My ol-vetter had such an acute memory, he could recite over one hundred songs from our High German *Lieder Buch* without missing a word.

"Ol-vetter always figured he would make a good leader," my father said. "He thought he could easily be a person who uses words to enlighten people."

Long long ago, in the days when old Samuel Hofer-vetter, who was about my ol-vetter's age and has been dead for almost ten years, was elected preacher, my ol-vetter volunteered to hand-copy the new preacher's sermon books. He had a steady hand; his handwriting didn't go all over the page like spiders' legs and it was easy to read. He wrote an extra copy for himself to study till the next opportunity came around for him to become a preacher.

"But Heaven Father must have had different plans for him," my ankela said. "Four times, when a preacher election came up, Ol-vetter's hopes were dashed because someone else pulled the "yes" note from the hat."

When Grandfather was about fifty or fifty-five years old, he wasn't working regularly with the men any more because there were plenty of younger men to keep everybody busy with the stocks and in the fields. That's when he started bonesetting. He'd given up his job as the carpenter a few years before and somehow he discovered that he had the right touch for making people's aches and pains in their bones go away, like his mother had had down in South Dakota. He seemed to know just the right way to massage the backbone and the shoulders to pull tension and misery from a person's body.

Of course, just being a bonesetter wasn't enough to keep him busy, so he'd still go and help out wherever his help was needed, like old Isaac Waldner and Kleinsasser Jakob-vetter did, who were some of the senior people in our colony. He'd help out with butchering pigs and cows, ducks, chickens and geese or help weigh and shovel off the grain trucks at harvest time. My ol-vetter had an old tattered book in which he had recorded the annual wheat and barley yields since even before 1946, when Old Lakeville colony branched out from Cypressville Colony by Medicine Hat, which is one of the oldest Lehreleut colonies in Alberta.

But before long he started having people from other colonies bring their pains for him to extract from their bones.

"That old Paul-vetter from Old Lakeville colony up by Moose Jaw, he really done my back a lot of good," people would spread the word around. Or they'd say: "Every time I visit him, that burning in my hip leaves me in peace for a long long time."

Sometimes a whole vanload or crewcab full of people from other colonies drove up to our colony to get doctored on by my grandfather. Even *Shmiedeleut* Hutterites from as far as Sioux Falls down in South Dakota came up to see him. And as well, a few English people from out in the world came regularly. A couple of times he had a few Amish men and women come on a bus. If my mind serves me right, they came from Iowa down in the States.

But still, at his age of about sixty, when he was too old already to be elected to the preacher job because there were plenty of younger baptised men available, my ol-vetter hadn't yet given up on his lifelong dream. He had kept all those sermon books he had hand-copied as a young man.

"Next time. Maybe next election they'll vote me to preacher," he said, his voice hopeful, knowing of course that his chances were very slim.

Actually, most men are glad when they end up not getting voted to the preacher position. Every time after preacher election you can see some relieved faces amongst the men. That's the job that carries the most responsibilities. If a preacher fails and sins he has much more to answer for to Heaven Father than someone with an ordinary job.

People have said often that my Michael Wipf-vetter from Prairieland colony by Swift Current should have been made a preacher for his own good. He's the kind of person who's very slack and he doesn't seem to care if he sins and laughs too much.

"It would be a blessing to his soul if he'd become a preacher," Hofer David-vetter our German school teacher says. "Then he'd have to lead by example and he wouldn't be able to tell his crazy jokes any more."

"How a man becomes a preacher is an act of Heaven Father," my father said to me and my brothers and sisters at the last election, when Andrew Hofer-vetter became the second preacher at Old Lakeville colony. "It doesn't matter how much or how little someone wishes to become the preacher, it doesn't even matter if the brothers casting the votes mentally try to get a certain brother elected to the job; ultimately the preacher position goes to the person who pulls the "yes" note from the hat after the brethren vote in the candidates."

I think my ol-vetter had given up on his dream of being a preacher already when Ankela died. That was two years before he died himself. By then he was walking with a cane already and he had a hard time shuffling up to the church house more than once a week in the summer. His body had become weak and thin because he had trouble with his blood; it kept disappearing. And in the end, he was so weak he had a hard time breathing.

But I still remember him, a year before he died, stubbornly hobbling along the gravel road to the blacksmith shop and the garages. He'd walk up behind us and quietly watch us pull wrenches on a tractor or cultivator. Sometimes it took ten minutes or longer till a person chanced to glance back and see Ol-vetter standing only six feet away. His blue eyes were alert as ever, taking in everything and he had his round black hat pushed down almost to his snowy eyebrows, covering his thin and pallid forehead.

"Elias, Elias, Elias," he'd say to me in his feeble voice. "You make sure that you stay in the colony and that whatever you do, even if it's just cutting the alfalfa or shovelling the manure, do it in Heaven Father's name and for the community. He'll reward you just the same."

Like I said before, my ol-vetter's last days aren't what stand out in my mind, even though it was only four months ago that he fell asleep to the Lord, as they say. To me, he was always a bonesetter. All those people that came to his funeral; all those trucks, vans, crewcabs and English cars, which made our colony look like the parking lot at the Town and Country Mall in Moose Jaw, were proof enough that he had had an important job. Yet it wasn't the kind of job that a person gets elected to, or the kind of job that makes a person seem real important or anything. Actually, it wasn't even considered a job. It's the kind of thing that just happens.